D1524047

AUTOPSY GONE WRONG

A Thriller

Preetinder Rahil

Copyright © 2022 Preetinder Rahil

All rights reserved.

This is a work of fiction. The characters, names, businesses, organizations, places, and events portrayed in this book are the products of the author's imagination or are used fictitiously. Any similarity to real persons, living or dead, events, locales, organizations, or businesses is coincidental and not intended by the author.

No part of this book may be reproduced, or stored in a retrieval system, or transmitted in any form or by any means, electronic, mechanical, photocopying, recording, or otherwise, without express written permission of the publisher except as allowed under the Copyright Law.

CONTENTS

CHAPTER 1

Today is not the day to be left indoors. It's a cracker of a day with a temperature of twenty-four degrees and a pleasant breeze and a clear blue sky. It's Friday afternoon and the start of a long weekend. Only an idiot would spend the time indoors. And yet here I am sitting in a room, staring at a dead body.

The room has no windows. The walls and the floor are pearl white, which makes even the tiniest bloodstain stick out like a sore thumb. It's eerily quiet here. The only thing I hear is my own breathing. I take slow deep breaths. I rub my hands in excitement. I know it's not good form to react like this in front of a dead body, but you see I love examining the dead. I have waited for this moment all my life. Maybe it's an exaggeration but it's not too far from the truth.

I got into medical school, not to heal the sick but to feel the dead. In my humble opinion, a dead body is far more interesting than a living one. There's a sense of mystery about it. There's a puzzle that needs to be solved, and who doesn't like solving puzzles? It's like reading a thriller, and I would take that any day over some literary masterpiece, which puts me to sleep more often than not. Conan Doyle over James Joyce any day.

A dead body is non-judgmental, and it tells you much more than what a living person has to offer. Ancient Egyptians knew the importance of dead bodies, and we are still in awe of the well-preserved mummies. If it was not for the pungent smell, I would gladly spend hours staring at the morbid details of a dead body. It won't complain. Even if I tell the whole story of my life, it will listen without blinking an eyelid!

It's not the story I told to the admissions committee at the medical school interview. It's no different than what politicians tell the gullible electorate and what desperate job seekers tell their prospective employers. I am not apologetic as someone must study the dead. Honesty is not always the best strategy, that's the bitter truth. If my dad had told during his medical residency interview that he wanted to be a doctor only to mint money, I am sure he would have been booted out. Yet that's what he does now: count his money as he shoves scopes in people's bottoms day in and day out. He knows his net worth to the last dollar.

I am on a two-week elective at the Institute of Forensic Sciences in Calgary. It was not easy to arrange. I had to dig up the past work of its director Dr. Gore and wrote an elaborate email listing his research papers and famous court cases and how much I was looking forward to working with him. Sucking up to those in power never fails. Boosting his ego was enough to land me this elective. The first few days were spent taking notes. I was disappointed. I am not here to push pencils; I am here to use scalpel and forceps. So, working on my first case is giddying me up.

I am as prepared as I can be. I am in full attire: scrubs, mask, gloves, the whole bit. I have Gray's Anatomy and Robbins Pathology to guide me. They are in my backpack which weighs ten pounds and is responsible for my sore back. But I am counting on my literary skills: Conan Doyle, Agatha Christie, et al. to give me the editorial edge so I can cut through the deluge of facts that may be coming my way.

It's critical that I make a good impression. My goal is clear: I want to be a forensic pathologist. I wouldn't say I always dreamt of being one since I was a little child or some cliché like that. But when I became a teenager, I soon realized that the only people who can do you harm are those who are alive. This created a fondness for the dead and the rest is history as they say. To achieve my goal, I need the blessings of Dr. Gore, specifically a strong letter of recommendation. It would make getting the few residency spots available in Anatomical Pathology a bit easier, but nothing is certain till the residency match day. I am only applying in this field and since you can count the number of residency positions on your fingers, the stakes are high.

Before I go into the nitty-gritty of the case at hand, I must first apologize for not formally introducing myself. I am Karan Inder Singh Sidhu, a fourth-year medical student from the University of Toronto. I have been called KISS, which I hate; calling me KIS Sidhu is not any better as it sounds the same. You can call me Karan. It's not the same as Karen. I am ready to get cracking. I will learn and improvise as I go along. Wish me luck.

CHAPTER 2

The unfortunate victim is a thirty-year-old man from Surrey BC. His name is Steve Hill. I check the body tag and the medical file to ensure it is the correct body. It's a simple but necessary step; I must follow the checklist to avoid any embarrassing mistakes. He was found dead at 8:40 AM today by a search and rescue team. He was reported missing by his girlfriend yesterday when he did not come back from a hike. They had gone to Banff, Alberta for a vacation.

His body was found seven kilometers northeast of Banff in a secluded area along the banks of the Bow River. He was lying on the side with his head smashed against the rock. The right side of the skull was open from the impact with the rock. There were no other signs of trauma. His backpack was missing and so was his cell phone. There are steep cliffs and dense forests all around the area where he was found. It was way off the hiking trails. The body was sent for further examination as the attending police officer deemed the death suspicious.

Where should I start? First things first, I need to make sure the guy is dead. It may seem silly, but mistakes do happen. I speak loudly into his ear, "Anyone there?" No response is reassuring. I shine light into his eyes and check his carotid pulse. Negative findings corroborate his dead status. I begin the head-to-toe exam, it's a safe bet. I don't want to rely on police notes as I will try to form an unbiased opinion if anything like that even exists. I did glance at the notes, but the handwriting was atrocious. It was an incomprehensible mess. I could only make out the word suspicious written in bold letters.

He is six feet one inch tall with a lean build, in keeping with his history of intense physical activity. The skull is fractured at multiple places. The scalp on the right side is barely hanging on. The dried blood is all over the scalp and behind the neck. I could see the brain matter through the skull opening. Whatever happened to him is stored somewhere in the brain but alas! there is no way of accessing that information now. I have seen the human brain in books and anatomical specimens, but this is the real deal. The site could have caused nausea and fainting in many but I only experience excitement and intrigue. I think I'm made for this kind of job.

I take the forceps and try to identify various parts of the brain for my own learning. I know it's selfish but that's how you learn. I could see no foreign objects, specifically no bullets or metallic debris in the scalp. I have the urge to keep going and open the skull up, but it is beyond my expertise, and I better get permission from Dr. Gore. I don't want to tamper with any evidence if it turns out to be a criminal case. Knowing one's limits is key to avoiding getting into trouble.

His arms are filled with tattoos. One tattoo says, "Live till you die," which aptly explains his present state. I examine every nook and corner of the body including the available orifices. It's a disgusting but unnecessary exam. There is nothing out of the ordinary except the left ankle. There are bruise marks on the left ankle forming a ring as if he had been tied with a rope. Bingo! I have a clue and it points to a possible criminal act. I'm excited to report this finding to Dr. Gore and earn some brownie points. The police must have noticed the same thing. I look at the police notes again, it's hopeless, I can't make out anything. I don't need validation from the police report, I can see the marks with my own eyes and that's good enough.

The guy is as stiff as a board. Rigor mortis is in full swing. He probably died early this morning or late at night, I don't want to commit to the exact time, it's beyond my pay grade. But that doesn't stop me from speculating about his death. I must weave some conspiracy theories and focus on the most probable one. I must let my imagination run wild, like an author almost. I could do that. In a criminal case, it's all about motive, motive, and motive. He was not rich and famous. He has no criminal record; I must check up on that. I need to call his girlfriend and ask for her alibi. They were traveling together. She has many questions to answer.

I must begin my investigative work in earnest. Time is of the essence in a criminal investigation. In medicine, we call it taking collateral information. It's less threatening than the word interrogation. I have been given the go ahead by Dr. Gore. He's the chief coroner and has broad investigative powers. I would exercise those powers on his behalf. It's time to go on a power trip. I'm excited. I would be subtle and non-confrontational. That should do the trick. Let's see.

CHAPTER 3

Lisa is a bartender and lives in Surrey, BC. She is currently staying in a hotel near the airport and is ready to fly back to BC once the mystery behind her boyfriend's death is cleared up. She showed very little emotion in front of the police. That's what I could gather from the police notes after much effort at deciphering the messy handwriting. She was possibly in emotional shock. Grief can present in different ways, one moment you are calm as a Yogi, another moment you burst like an overflowing dam. I don't want to be the one at the receiving end, but it may reveal her character and perhaps her motives.

I call the cell phone. It's ringing and ringing. I hate leaving a voicemail.

"Hi! This is Lisa. Did you miss me? If you did, please leave a voicemail and I will get back to you if I like what I hear, Bye!"

Interesting. Even a voicemail can tell us something about a person. But the voicemail is not good enough. I want her, in a non-romantic way, you know what I mean. There's only one thing left to do: keep calling, like a stalker. I call the second time, and it goes to voicemail again, bummer. The third time it's ringing and finally, she picks up.

"Hello," Lisa says. It is a hello said with a question mark. She is suspicious and understandably so. The call ID is blocked from the hospital, so she doesn't know who is calling.

"Hi! Is this Lisa?" I ask my own question.

"Yes!" It is another response that possibly ends with a question than an answer.

"Can I take one or two minutes of your most valuable time?"

"Sorry, I'm not in the right frame of mind to buy anything or answer any survey."

"Before you hang up, I must tell you I am calling from the Institute of Forensic Sciences. I am calling regarding Steve Hill."

"Oh."

"I am so sorry for your loss. I know you are going through a difficult time." A bit of empathy doesn't hurt.

"Thank you."

"I am Karan, a medical student working with Dr. Gore, who is the chief coroner. We are investigating the circumstances around Steve's untimely death. And you are the best person to shed some light on the matter."

"I was not with him. I don't know what happened. I have already told the police. Didn't you read the notes?" She is throwing questions rather than answers at me.

"I have read the notes alright. But to put them in the right perspective there is no better alternative than talking to you directly. I hope you don't mind."

"So, what do you want to know?" Another rhetorical question.

"Well, what brought you to Banff?"

"It's a tourist town, it's summer, and we love the Rockies."

"Is it your first time here?"

"Yes."

"And how do you like it?"

"It was a picture-perfect vacation until it ended with a nightmare."

"I know, this is not how you want to end your vacation. How long have you guys been together?"

"We met on a hike in Annapurna, Nepal two years ago. It was love at first sight. I still remember that day. He saved me from falling off the cliff. He held my hand and didn't let it go. But when he needed help..." She starts crying.

"I am sorry. You guys were pros. Going to Annapurna is not a walk in the park."

"Thank you. We are not mountain climbers, just hikers. But it's tough to hike in the Himalayas."

"How was he?"

"He was the most loving and big-hearted guy I have ever met. He was full of life and treated danger as his second girlfriend."

"A daredevil?"

"He took risks, but he was not stupid. We all take risks, don't we?"

"You are absolutely right." I use validation as bait.

"Ask me anything." It worked.

"How was his health?"

"Perfect. He was obsessed with fitness. He could miss a meal but not his exercise routine."

"Any drug or alcohol problems?"

"Drugs and exercise don't go together, do they? I don't want to lie; he had his share of addictions, but he buried his past and never looked back."

"Any family?"

"He came from a dysfunctional family. He had not spoken to his parents for years. He grew up in foster homes. He was always running away from his past. Maybe that's why he became a hiker."

"You may be right. Why did he go for a hike alone?"

"I am embarrassed to say that I tripped on a sidewalk. I was limping and in no position to go for a hike. Steve was disappointed. We always went together. We only had a few days in Banff, and he wanted to make the most of it. He was hesitant to leave me alone in the hotel, but I prodded him to go and have a good time. I wish I hadn't."

"It's not your fault, you didn't know what fate had in store. Hindsight is 20/20. What time did he leave the hotel?"

"We had breakfast at the hotel together and he left soon after. It must have been around ten o'clock. He packed food and other essentials and kissed me goodbye, and he was gone." She is sobbing again.

I pause, give her time to gather herself. "Did he tell where he was going?"

"He had plans to go to Johnston Caves and then take one of the hiking trails."

"So how did he end up where he was found?"

"I don't know."

"When did you know something was wrong?"

"He should have come by the evening. I called his cell at four o'clock, but it was switched off. When I did not hear back from him by eight o'clock and it was getting dark, I panicked. It was at that time I made a call to the police."

"And what did they say to you?"

"The police reassured me that they would send a search and rescue party and would keep me informed."

"And when did you find out about his death?"

"The police called me this morning and gave me the unpleasant news. They showed me his body virtually and it was the most horrible moment of my life."

"What did you do when he was away?"

"So, you want to know my whereabouts? Am I under suspicion? I told the police that I was at the hotel all the time. I could barely walk, what else could I do? You guys have no empathy. You don't know how it feels to lose a loved one."

"I'm sorry if I hurt your feelings but I had to ask that question. You would have done the same thing if you were in my shoes."

"Have you done the autopsy yet?"

"That would be Dr. Gore's decision. Do you have a hypothesis of what really happened?"

"I don't know what to say. It doesn't make sense. Steve was such a good hiker. Accidents do happen. Maybe he was in the wrong place at the wrong time. Before he left, he asked me if I would miss him if he didn't come back. At that time, I thought he was just joking but those words haunt me now."

"Are you saying that he killed himself?"

"No! He was not depressed. He often joked about his death. He knew he took risks in life and one day maybe those risks would get the better of him and they did."

"I won't take any more of your time. You have been most helpful."

"When would you release the body?"

"I will discuss the case with Dr. Gore. We will let you know soon. Thank you for your cooperation. Bye for now."

I don't know if she's telling the truth. I couldn't look into her eyes. That's the disadvantage of talking on the phone. You miss all the nonverbal cues. She sounds genuine. I have no reason to doubt her. I would take her answers at face value. Let's see what the police officer has to say.

CHAPTER 4

I don't like talking to the police. There is a sense of anxiety that comes upon me when dealing with law enforcement. Maybe because I belong to the minority community. Maybe I've seen too many cop thrillers with dirty cops. I have done nothing wrong here and I am working on the behalf of law enforcement. So, I should be OK, right? But I still feel a bit nervous. I need to gather my thoughts before I call the cop. The police officer who signed the report is Dean Webb. I call his cell number. Hope he picks up and then my job will be done.

The cell rings and on the second ring the officer picks up. "This is officer Dean Webb; how can I help you?" He has a commanding voice suitable for a police officer.

"Hi, thanks for taking my call. I am Karan, a medical student working with Dr. Gore. I'm calling regarding the death of Steve Hill. I hope you can shed some light on it."

"There is nothing much to add besides what I wrote on the police notes. Are you guys going to do the autopsy?"

"Will see. It's up to Dr. Gore. How did you find Steve?"

"We used the police drone. It's a neat technology, isn't it? It makes our job a bit easier."

"Sure, it does."

"The poor guy was dead, and it was clear that he fell off the cliff. The question is why and how? His backpack was missing. His cell phone was nowhere to be found. Why?"

"Did you look for those things?"

"Yes, we did the drone search, but nothing was found. There is dense forest all around. There's a lot of smog due to forest fires, so it's not easy to do the search."

"What about ground search?"

"We don't have time and personnel to do that kind of an operation. We already found the guy. There's no justification for that kind of an expense."

"Why did you deem the death as suspicious?"

"It's the protocol. It's safer to leave the decision to the coroner. And there is something sinister about Steve and his girlfriend's background."

"Really! You didn't put that in the report?"

"It's a conjecture and I didn't want to make it official. Steve had several convictions for arson. His girlfriend Lisa has declared bankruptcy several times and has been convicted of shoplifting. Not ideal citizens, are they?"

"How do their backgrounds play a role here?"

"I don't know. Maybe not, but it's something to think over."

"Do you think his girlfriend killed him?" I ask bluntly.

"How?" The officer says in a shrill tone.

"Maybe she hired a hitman to do the job."

"You have the most fertile imagination. It's possible but it's far-fetched." The officer is trying to control his laughter.

"What are your next steps?"

"If Dr. Gore decides that it's an accident, then that's the end of it. We won't pursue it separately."

"Thank you, officer. You've been most helpful."

"You're welcome."

I believe I got the scoop. Both Lisa and Steve have juicy backgrounds. Are they relevant to his untimely death? That's the million-dollar question. Is Steve responsible for any of the forest fires? If he is, that would be something. Maybe he had some accomplices. Maybe they had a fight, and he was pushed over the cliff. Maybe it's a case of a drug deal gone wrong. That's why his backpack is missing. No one is taking that line of thought. No one searched for any other persons. The police resources are overstretched with forest fires. The murderer can easily fly under the radar.

If I'm able to convince Dr. Gore that it's a

suspicious death, then maybe the police will begin the investigation and commit resources to find more evidence. It would be a sensational case. There would be press conferences and I may be lucky enough to attend one of them. It would boost my resume to the stratosphere. Currently, these are some random thoughts. I'm not sure how Dr. Gore will react to this. I don't want to come out as stupid in front of him. I will give him the facts without committing to any opinion.

I put my findings in the form of a written report. It would come in handy when I verbalize my findings. If Dr. Gore agrees with my findings, then the next step would be to do an autopsy. My hands are itching to cut open the body. I'm eager to grab his heart, literally. I'm ready to put my dissection skills into practice. I hope all goes well.

CHAPTER 5

Dr. Gore travels in an entourage. It's not a presidential motorcade but it's no less impressive. He travels with a team consisting of nurses, medical students, and other staff. He walks fast and others have a hard time catching up to him. I guess this is the problem with all successful people. They're all type-A personalities and always on the go. Walking is also a competitive sport for them.

I hear the tapping noise of shoes. The entourage of Dr. Gore is arriving. He is the first to open the door. He has a commanding personality. He's at least six feet tall with a muscular build. He must be in his 60s. He has grey hair. He has a French beard. I think he puts oil in his hair as the hair are immaculately combed and shiny. He's wearing a white overcoat as usual. It has no stains whatsoever but the same could not be said about his character. His ID badges clip to the front pocket of his coat. He has a Mont Blanc pen in his front pocket. You can't miss the Rolex Submariner even from a distance. He is wearing Ray-Ban glasses that are gold-plated. He stares through them like a sniper and it's intimidating. When he looks at you, he doesn't blink, and the onus is on you to lower your gaze. His leather shoes are shiny enough to see one's reflection. And he wears a bow tie.

I stand up from my chair and give a customary bow and say," Good morning, Sir." I guess colonial submissiveness is ingrained in my mind and it would take several generations to get rid of it. I say it so softly that he ignores it.

He puts his six-pound hand on my shoulders like a mafia boss. "How are you, young man?" It's a rhetorical question but I must give an enthusiastic response.

"Couldn't be better, Sir."

"This is Karan, a medical student from the University of Toronto. He wants to follow in my footsteps to become a forensic pathologist." Dr. Gore introduces me to his team of new recruits. They nod with a meek smile.

"Are you ready with the case, Karan?"

"Yes, Sir," I answer like a soldier.

"Good. Before we go into the case, has anyone seen an autopsy or for that matter a dead body before?"

"I have seen my grandmother's body," the nursing student says. Her ID badge says, Daisy Smith. She's taller than me. Guys don't like girls taller than them. It hurts their ego. Maybe she's wearing high heels. I look down. She's not.

Bummer.

"That doesn't count." There is a lack of empathy in Dr. Gore's voice. "How would you know if a person has died?"

"I will shake the person, shine light into the eyes, and check the pulse," the medical student says. He's Jim from UBC. I have met him before. He's gunning for plastic surgery, so this rotation is sort of like a vacation for him. He is not my competitor. And he's not taller than me, which is a bonus.

"And?" Dr. Gore asks.

"Oh! check the temperature."

"Good. Can anyone tell me what's the most common cause of death?"

"Cardiac arrest," Daisy says.

"So, you mean to say that a person's heart stops before he dies. You could say the same thing about his breathing and thinking. Isn't it?"

Daisy realizes that she may have spoken out of turn. She keeps mum, which is a wise choice.

"A certificate of death is the final document in a person's history. It must be accurate. Be specific. Like coronary artery disease or congestive heart failure, not that someone's heart stopped."

Everyone nods as if the president is giving the State of Union address.

"Let's say the death is suspicious. We don't know how a person died. We want to know more. We open the chest with a saw and look for the heart and it's not there. What would you do?"

This time the silence is deafening.

"Anyone? Jim?"

"Maybe he had a congenital condition?"

"So, you mean to say that he could survive all these years without a heart?"

Jim looks down. I like the embarrassed look on his face.

"Daisy?"

"Maybe someone took away his heart or maybe he's an alien?"

"Be specific."

"A Martian?"

I want to laugh but I don't' because my turn is coming, and I have no idea if my answer would be equally stupid.

"It's your turn Karan, I have high hopes from you."

It's not good the pressure is on me. I must think fast. I'll make an educated guess. "Maybe we should look on the other side of the chest."

"Bingo. What do you call that?"

"Dextrocardia?"

"Are you answering or asking?"

"Both."

"Good job. Yes, you always look for variations in the human body."

I am beaming with pride. I look around to see their faces. They have a poker expression. No smiles. No thumbs up. Jealous, maybe. I don't care.

Dr. Gore's pager buzzes. He looks at the pager and ignores it like a true boss. I wish I was in his position. My time will come someday.

CHAPTER 6

We spread all around the body as if performing a ritual. Dr. Gore is standing opposite me. He uncovers the body. The naked dead body doesn't feel any shame, nor does Dr. Gore. He gives precedence to education over human decency.

"Karan let's start with the case. Salient features only, no stories."

"The body is that of Steve Hill. He was a thirty-year-old man from Surrey BC. He was vacationing with his girlfriend Lisa in Banff. He went on a hike alone yesterday morning. He was reported missing by his girlfriend last night when he failed to return and did not answer his calls. His body was found by the police at 8:40 am today on the outskirts of Banff on the banks of the Bow River. His right head was smashed against the rock presumably by falling off a cliff. Rigor mortis was beginning to set in when he was found. His past medical history is non-contributory. He had a remote drug and alcohol abuse history. He was physically active and a professional hiker. He was estranged from his family and had a traumatic childhood but there were no current mental health concerns. He was convicted of arson in the past. His backpack and cell phone are missing. The drone search of the area did not find anything. The collateral was taken from his girlfriend Lisa and the on-duty police officer, who sent the body for possible biopsy as the death was deemed suspicious."

"Hmm. And your exam findings."

"There is an open comminuted fracture of the parietal and temporal bones on the right side. The brain parenchyma is visible. There is dried blood over the neck and face. There are possible closed neck fractures. There are no other visible signs of trauma except there is a concentric ring of bruises along the left ankle. Rigor mortis has set in."

"Impression?"

"Steve Hill was a 30-something unfortunate man who died of blunt trauma to the head. The circumstances surrounding his death remain suspicious. The next course of action is to conduct an autopsy."

I feel a great deal of weight has been lifted off my shoulders. My job is done. Dr. Gore has a smile on his face. It's not a good sign. It's a sarcastic smile and I have been at the receiving end of plenty of them.

"How would an autopsy solve this mystery?"

"There may be injuries that are currently undetected and may be responsible for his death.

He could have been intoxicated."

"There may be secondary injuries. So, what! He most probably fell off a cliff. I highly doubt that any secondary injuries would add anything of substance. You said that he had no addictions, so why would we do a toxicology analysis?"

I see smiles all around. Jealousy.

"There is evidence of foul play. The bruises around his ankle may have been caused by a rope tied around his leg. Maybe he has been dragged off the cliff."

"By whom?"

"I don't know. Maybe a drug deal went wrong or a serial killer perhaps."

"There is no circumstantial evidence to support any of your theories."

Dr. Gore takes out a lens from his front coat pocket and examines the bruises around the ankle. It doesn't take too long for him to conclude.

My eyes are fixated on him. I am desperately seeking approval.

"The bruises are not from a rope but from the ankle being caught in a tree branch as he fell."

My ego is deflated. I have lost my case. I feel dejected. I don't say anything. It's better to swallow one's pride than to spit it out.

"Don't worry young man. You presented your case with tact and vigor. It's not about right and wrong. It's about the process and developing some reasoning. Good job."

It's nice to finally hear some encouraging

words. I am out of the penalty box. But that doesn't take away my huge disappointment at not being able to do the autopsy.

I am pulled to one side by Dr. Gore. He wants to have a private conversation with me. I'm nervous. I'm not sure what's coming my way. I don't think I have committed any blunder.

"Let me be honest, I would have leaned towards doing an autopsy as well but today is not a good day to do an autopsy. Today is the gala night of the medical association and I'm being awarded the lifetime achievement award. I can't miss that. You have my permission to do an informal autopsy but only open the brain that's easily accessible to you. You have two hours before the folks from the morgue take the body away. I know it's not the ideal outcome for you, but I hope you learn something and if you have any questions, you can ask me later. How does that sound?"

"Sounds good."

I got a consolation prize, that's ok. I will make the best of it. Dr. Gore and his army of subordinates march away. I hear whispers, maybe they are gossiping about me. I am sensitive that way. I don't care, I repeat ten times. It's a therapy that works sometimes.

CHAPTER 7

I am all alone with the body, it's showtime. I take a scalpel in one hand and blunt forceps in the other. I wonder if Steve was afraid of injections and giving blood samples, but I don't expect any reaction from him today as I rip his brain apart. It's a mess. It's not easy to identify structures. I have the textbook of gross anatomy open. The brain looks nothing like what's shown in the pictures of the Atlas. I get my hands dirty as I cut and pull through the brain tissue. I could feel the texture of the brain. I am beginning to identify the limbic system and the brain stem. His secrets and memories are all buried there. If we could squeeze out information like getting honey from a honeycomb, it would serve humanity well.

I have always been fascinated by eyes. They are as complex as the brain. I follow the optic nerve to the eyeball like following an HDMI cable to the router. It's not easy, there are entanglements along the way.

I see a green bump on the back of the eyeball.

It's tiny. I can't make out what's going on. Is it a tumor?

I get the magnifying glass, it's a bulla or a bubble in layman's terms. It is pulsating. What the heck?

I touch it with blunt forceps, but there is some resistance. It has fluid in it. Should I pop it? You know the answer. Of course, I would. How can I leave it alone? If I don't then who else will? It's my only chance as soon his body will be gone forever.

I have a gauze in one hand to prevent any spills though I don't expect much fluid to come out from a tiny bubble. And of course, I'm wearing gloves. I press the scalpel against the bubble. As soon as I touch it, it pops.

The fluid under pressure comes out like a coiled spring and hits my both eyes with great force. Like a sniper hitting the target. My eyes burn. Damn it. How could I be so stupid? Why didn't I wear safety glasses? I know they fog over due to the surgical mask, and I had no choice but to put them aside. I couldn't see a damn thing and so I took the risk. What have I done?

I don't think I would go blind. It's organic tissue, not some acid. But why are my eyes burning so much? I can't see anything. I would rather die than go blind. My career would be over. My girlfriend would leave me. Then what would be the point of living? I'm drowning in negative thoughts.

I need to get a handle on the situation. OK,

I need to take deep breaths. I need water. The water bottle is in my bag. I kept it in the locker room. It has a passcode. Damn it. Why do we need passcodes for everything these days? One can't even drink water without putting in a passcode. Let me call for help. Shoot! My cell phone is on charging in the locker room. Maybe I'll go out and ask for help. I don't think it would be of much use either. It's Friday afternoon. The corridors of the institute are dead even on weekdays. If I get locked out of the room, I would be stranded in the corridor.

It's the worst day of my life and it's not even over yet. I can't stand still. My anxiety has ignited a fire inside me. I don't need the fire brigade; I need reassurance to extinguish it. I put my hands on the wall and try to go across to the exit door and maybe someone will hear my call for help. I take one step at a time. I take twenty steps without bumping into something. I'm not sure where I am in relation to the door.

Ouch! My head has hit a sharp object, maybe a shelf. I don't need any more trouble. I check for any bleeding. The good news is it's dry. My head hurts. I hope it's not another concussion. I get a concussion every time I play sports. I had concussions playing baseball, ice hockey, and cricket. I have given up on sports altogether. And I still get a concussion. It's called bad luck. Maybe it's just a tension headache.

Why is my vision not coming back? My body

is shivering with fear. I have got an idea, why don't I cry. Tears are water, they are natural and good for the eyes. Why didn't I think of it earlier? Better late than never. It's not too hard to cry the way my day is going. I have cried vigorously watching sitcoms, giving into fake emotions shown on the television.

The tears pour down my eyes like a torrential downpour. It should clean up the green fluid in my eyes. I wait and pray.

The fog is beginning to clear. I can see. Thank God. There is a reddish hue to my vision. I don't mind that. I'm relieved that I can see something. Vision is one of those things that we take for granted, like oxygen. Ask any mountaineer who has been to the death zone climbing 8000-meter peaks. Oxygen is the most valuable commodity up there. I don't intend to be that adventurous. I will take 20/20 vision any day over six-pack muscles.

I look around. I was nowhere near the exit door. I was wasting my time going to the far-end corner of the room. I was navigating without any guideposts and the result was predictable. The room is big enough to host a small party. It has eleven-foot ceilings and enough pot lights to give anyone a migraine. I see the shelf that I bumped against. It has sharp corners. I am lucky that I didn't hit my head against the sharp corner, otherwise, I would have had a big laceration on my scalp. The shelf has antique books on it. The ones in which they teach family doctors to do an appendectomy. The books are from the '50s and '60s. These days family doctors hesitate to suture a simple laceration. Those were the days.

I go back to the dissection table. I want to see what happened to the green bubble. I look at the body and my jaw drops.

There is no skin on the body. I can see the internal organs in detail. It's uncanny. How is it possible? I rub my eyes. I open and close my eyes in quick succession. I knock on my head. Maybe my brain needs a kick. I'm not talking about coffee people. I tilt my head in amazement like a cute dog. It only results in more amazement. I can see through the muscles and into the organs and the bony structures. My head is like a dial. I can fine-tune the imagery and cut through the layers of the human body in thin slices.

It's unbelievable. I don't know what to make of it. Is it a curse? A possession perhaps? Or is there a scientific explanation? Maybe that green fluid altered the retinal structure of my eyes. None of it makes any sense.

I put my hand over my eyes in exhaustion. There is no skin on my fingers, just a bunch of tendons wrapped around the bones. This can't be happening. I run to the locker room and look in the mirror.

I look like a ghost. It's scary. I'm alive but in the mirror, I look like a cadaver. I stare at the mirror for ten long minutes. It's not unheard of in the world of fashion but it's new to me. I have always avoided looking at my face for too long as I only see my crooked nose, acne scars, and occasional grey hair.

I now have a whole different perspective of what's wrong with my body. I see polyps behind my nose that make me snore at night. No wonder my girlfriend is not excited about sharing the bed with me. I see a chain of lymph nodes around my neck. They form a necklace of pearls around my neck. What I don't see is any problem with my eyes. The eyeballs appear normal and the retinal layer along with the macula is clean. I am no ophthalmologist, but I can spot obvious abnormalities as I have seen enough pictures of eye anatomy.

I look down and see more horror. The dangling genitalia is awkward looking. I can see urine flowing from the kidneys to the bladder. I can see undigested food bits in my gut. Yuck!

Who says knowledge is a gift? In this case, it's a curse. I have become a walking CT scan. Thinking of that, am I radioactive? If I am, that's no good. It's a recipe for all things cancerous. I need to get myself medically checked. There is another plausible explanation. Maybe I am delusional. There's only one way to find out. If I see something inside my body and it turns out to be true on subsequent diagnostic imaging then it's not a fluke, it's a miracle. It's a power that I have been bestowed on. It's up to me what I do with it.

CHAPTER 8

It's time to say goodbye to Steve. I don't know what he was up to, but I have gotten tangled with his fate. The morgue people are coming soon. I need to prepare the body for their arrival. I look at the eyeballs for any remnants of the green bubble. There are none, apart from some slough on the optic nerve. I put together the scalp bones with the help of the stapler. I can still see his internal organs and can't resist the urge to grab them. I reach out for them but am met by resistance from the invisible skin as if they're wrapped inside a transparent sheet. I have had enough. I put the cover on the body. I pray for his soul. It's a decent thing to do. Maybe I will get the secondary benefit. I look at the body one more time before shutting the door.

The corridors are bright but quiet. If I shout, I can hear my echo. The building has many wings and I'm in the red wing appropriate for the autopsy department. The walls have portraits of physicians' past and present, mostly old white people. Their subtle smiles tease me. I want to follow in their footsteps and maybe one day my picture will also hang on these walls, hopefully before I die.

I'm in desperate need of a washroom. Stress induces the bladder and it's on the verge of overflowing. I can see the bladder valves trying their best to control a dam that's going to burst. Why is it so difficult to find washrooms in a hospital? There's nobody to ask. I am new here. I am not familiar with the layout of the place. Finally, I see a washroom sign and I keep on going for at least seven minutes. The corridors are never-ending as if I'm in an airport terminal. Just ahead sign is a trap, it should be far ahead. I brisk walk as running may cause leakage. The washroom is clean but still smells like a hospital washroom. I do my thing and I'm proud that I'm able to squeeze the last drop of urine from my bladder.

The next project is to find stairs. I see the elevators, but I don't want to take the risk. I have this irrational fear of elevators. What if it breaks down? No one will help me for hours. It's a long weekend. The way my day has gone it's a reasonable assumption.

I go to the cafeteria. There is hardly anyone in the cafeteria. The employees outnumber the clients by three to one. I order coffee with cream. There isn't much choice in the food. Donuts and bread are a few hours away from being thrown away. I choose croissant, a safe choice. It is sticky and cold like my day.

I see people walking around with their internal organs exposed. When you see someone naked, where would you first look? Be honest. I tell you, dangling genitalia without the skin is a horror show. I have no desire to see someone's ovaries or testicles in detail. It's a whole new world for me and it's not pretty. We're so used to seeing people with skin. The lack of it makes people look like ghosts and zombies.

I want to talk to someone. I could call my parents and my girlfriend. But I hesitate. They will press the panic button which won't help anyone. They are far away. I don't need advice; I need empathy which I'm sorry to say no one provides. People just want to impose their viewpoints. I want patient listening. Maybe I'll talk to myself in the mirror with my eyes closed of course. Don't worry I will speak to myself in the privacy of my room otherwise gazing eyes won't be kind to me. They would think I have gone mental. People pass judgment on others faster than kindness. It should be the other way around but that's the world we live in.

When you are a medical student, your day doesn't end at 5:00 PM. It may be the end of one shift, but another is about to begin. My day is not over. I'm on call in the ER. No sleep tonight. There are work rules for medical students, but they are more often broken than observed. A lowly medical student like me better not utter a word. One bad review from my supervisor would stick on me like a badly done tattoo on the face.

I have a room in the student dormitory but it's one block away. I don't have the energy to go back and forth. A short nap in the on-call room is all I can muster.

I stretch my legs on the sofa in the call room. A couple of staff doctors come by to collect their mail. They must be thinking, been there, done that. Poor guy. They don't know that I know more about their bodies than they do. My smile is proportionate and genuine.

I toss and turn waiting for sleep to arrive. It comes unannounced.

I am being dragged. My feet are tied. I'm in pain. The surface is rough. I'm in the woods somewhere. I don't know who's pulling me. I cry for help. No one is there to help me. I know that the end is near.

Should I pray or fight? I do neither. I'm overwhelmed by the situation. My life flashes before me. It's my last chance to introspect; how I lived my life and what I learned from this human experience.

I am dangling at the edge of a cliff. The drop is steep. The chance of survival is none. Gravity is ruthless. I can calculate the speed at which I'll strike the ground. I do understand that gravity is merely the curvature of spacetime. But these intellectual shenanigans won't save me.

My feet are beginning to slip from the rope.

The countdown to inevitable fall has begun. My skull would be smashed, and brain matter would pop out like a crushed coconut. My body would become fodder for wildlife. I begin to fall. The heart is sinking. I strike the ground but I'm still alive.

How is that possible? I bounce back from the ground as if a transparent layer is covering the ground and acting as a trampoline. Maybe I'm in a dream. But it all feels too real to be a dream. I'm confused, which increases the probability of a dream.

I open my eyes. I rub my eyes and look around. The call room is empty, but my mind is not. I check my body parts. They are intact. I can still see my internal organs. The sleep didn't change anything. I am stuck with this curse. I had a nightmare, but it wasn't much worse than what I'm living through. Does this dream mean anything? I don't have a crystal ball, but I do have time to wait and see.

CHAPTER 9

It's a full moon. The ER is packed. No place to sit, there are stretchers in the hallways. Welcome to hallway medicine. I don't know why people decide to get sick on the weekend when all other doctor offices are closed. They all flood to the ER and expect prompt service. Today's wait time is five hours. It's proudly displayed on the computer bulletin in the waiting room to set the expectations low. People are frustrated and angry but not in panic. They know something will be done but just don't know when. Staff are burnt out. The niceties and formalities become victims. It must be hard, thank you for waiting, these phrases drain too much energy. Tell your problem, not your story is the motto.

The ER is divided into four parts: pediatric, ambulatory, acute, and locked-in psychiatric unit. Pediatric ER has its own waiting room. It's full of crying and nervous children. There are small cubicles with curtains. Privacy is a nonstarter. There is one procedure room where a noncompliant kid could get restrained. The screams stay inside. Today is the day of runny noses and coughs. There is almost rhythm and rhyme to their sneezes and coughs. I don't want to catch a cold. I would skip the pediatric ER today. At least that's the plan.

A narrow hallway takes you to the ambulatory part of the ER. It's hit and miss. You have run-of-the-mill back pains and colds, but you could also see complex medical syndromes. It's a place to pour your bookish knowledge onto your mentors and gain some brownie points.

The acute side of the ER is a place where ambulances bring the sickest of the sick. Time is of the essence and things happen fast. High adrenaline stuff. It's a place where you need good abs because chest compressions are no less exhausting than a bench press in a gym. I like this place but only in doses. You can learn a lot without the added burden of responsibility.

The locked-in psychiatric unit of the ER is a no-go zone for medical students. Thank God. Who wants to interview someone high on crystal meth? Staff frequently get punched. I'm scared of that place. The psychiatry residents deal with the perpetual chaos. I admire them but I don't envy them.

The heart of the ER is the central station. It's the command centre. Staff doctors sit there to complete their notes, check labs, and order tests. It's all electronic but some old schoolers still carry pen and paper. It's also a place to gossip, crack jokes, and throw smiles. It's a survival instinct. A depressed doctor is not what you want. There is death and sickness all around, but you still must keep your spirits up. So, if you hear sounds of laughter, don't judge.

I'm hanging out with Dr. Richards today. He's a cool dude. He's six feet tall with a good physique. Somehow, I always get tall mentors with towering personalities. His biceps pop out of his scrubs. It's my second shift with him. He allows me to go anywhere in the ER and do whatever I want. Learn, learn, and learn but not burn, that's his style. I like that. He calls his ER unit the dream team and I would agree with that. Nurses flirt with him and vice versa but I intend to keep a strictly professional relationship with him. I keep my boundaries clear. I don't let border disputes arise.

I browse the computer. I use one finger to type. I never learned to type fast. My typing speed is abysmal. Dictation is a lifesaver.

"Why do you use only one hand? What do you do with the other hand?" I hear a voice from behind.

It's Dr. Richards. I wouldn't have recognized him without the skin. His voice and ID badge were enough for identification.

I stand up and give him a meek smile.

"I'm serious, what do you do with the other hand?" His sarcastic smile hides the double meaning talk.

I must come up with something quick, "Ahh, it's a habit."

"Not a good one."

"Quite."

"Are you ready for an exciting night?"

"Yes I am." It's a lie but I say it with the conviction of a lawyer.

"I want you to start in the pediatrics area and do at least one case in each unit."

"It's all coughs and colds over there."

"If you can digest bread and butter, only then you'll appreciate the gravy."

I have no choice. I head to the pediatric waiting room which is nothing but a petri dish of viruses.

I do a quick scan of the room. Almost everyone has a runny nose. I see a small girl with a huge spleen. That's not normal. I call the patient.

Jenny is a six-year-old with a sore throat and fever. She and her mom come to the cubicle. They're happy to be called after a long wait.

"Hi, I am Karan. I'm a medical student. Do you mind if I ask you a few questions?"

"Go ahead," her mom says.

"So, what brings you here today?"

"Jenny has had a fever and sore throat for two days. It's the fourth time in the last two months. She never got that many colds before. It's not the flu season. It's the middle of summer. We have been to the family doctor and urgent care clinic. All they say is to wait it out. I'm sick of it."

"I can understand your frustration but it's sensible advice."

"But it's not working. Something is wrong."

"I can see that."

"See what?" An angry parent is a medical student's nightmare.

I can't tell what I see. She will freak out. I need to come up with a medical explanation.

"Your worry is valid. We need to run some tests to make sure there is no underlying medical illness that would explain recurrent illness."

"See, someone listens." She has a tear in her eyes.

The girl is nervous but cooperative. I do a quick exam. I don't need to run my hands along her neck to feel for any lymph nodes. I can just see that they're big. I do a percussion test to check for an enlarged spleen. It's redundant but it's good for practice.

I order a stat blood count. I ask them to wait and reassure them that it won't be too long.

I brush up on the causes of enlarged spleen. I'm suspecting leukemia.

Dr. Richards comes to me.

"I got a critical result call from the lab. Did you order blood work on this kid?"

"Yes, I did." I give him the background information on the clinical case.

"Good job. You may be right. I think this may be acute myeloid leukemia. Let's consult pediatrics. She needs to be admitted. Do you mind talking to the parents?"

"I will tell the mom."

Breaking bad news is never easy. It's better done in doses. Avoid sudden shock.

"We have the blood work results. Jenny's white blood count is quite low."

"What does that mean?" Her voice is trembling.

"It could mean many things. Infection can do that and so can a blood disorder. A child specialist will come and check her. We need more tests to come to a diagnosis."

"Should I be worried?"

"You already are. She may have a serious blood disorder. I don't want to jump the gun. Let's wait for more tests."

"Thank you for your help. You would become a good doctor."

I hate this part of the job. To tell someone that their young child has a life-threatening illness is gut-wrenching. But someone must do it. I think I did alright. What do you think?

CHAPTER 10

This x-ray vision is something. It's not a fluke. What I saw has been validated by a scientific lab test. It's a superpower that I've got. The possibilities are limitless.

I roam around in ambulatory care. It's Friday night so plenty of aches and pains after spirited fights.

I mumble, "That's a fracture. That's not. That one is. That one isn't."

My self-confidence is soaring. I do a proud walk. It's midnight but I'm not sleepy. I can run a sprint.

Code blue, code blue. The announcement on the intercom is loud and clear. I run. So does Dr. Richards. The rest of the central station carries on with their work. It's a routine affair for them and they mind their own business.

The resuscitation room can accommodate twenty people. There are seven people in the room including me. It's plenty. Any more would make a crowd. The patient bed is at the centre of the room. It is surrounded by all kinds of resuscitation equipment. Expensive and delicate. A male nurse is doing chest compressions on the patient.

The paramedic gives the history. It's a forty-something male who called 911 half an hour ago. He was roaming in the mall when he experienced shortness of breath. He was on his way to the hospital when he collapsed in the courtyard of the emergency room. The medical history is non-contributory. He is not on any medications. He had never been sick apart from coughs and colds.

"How many minutes of chest compressions?" Dr. Richards yells.

"Five minutes," yells the paramedic.

"Keep going."

"Is he going to make it?" I ask.

"Not likely. Probably a myocardial infarction. May have to call the coroner. He would need an autopsy. It's right up your alley."

"I hope it doesn't come to that."

"Hope is not a strategy."

I'm a bystander as the medical team continues its resuscitation efforts. The defibrillator is used, and epinephrine is injected. The cardiac monitor shows a flatline. Not good.

I come closer to the body and scan it from top to bottom. I can't find anything wrong with his organs, but I don't have a good view of the heart. The chest compressions are obstructing my view.

"You fancy some chest compressions?" Dr. Richards asks.

"Sure." It's also a lie. But not a complete lie. My body says no but my mind says hell yeah.

I climb on the table and over the patient. I interlock my fingers to form a firm grip for chest compressions. I now have a clear view of the heart. I can see what's wrong. The heart is drowning in the pericardial fluid. The outer layer of the heart is filled with fluid. It's not allowing the heart to contract.

"Dr. Richards, can I do pericardiocentesis?"

"Why?" Dr. Richard looks surprised.

"It's worth trying. Chest compressions are not working."

"Have you done it before?"

"Only on a dummy patient."

"Go ahead. If you make a mistake no one would ever know," Dr. Richard throws a smile.

I take the aspiration needle. I don't need to worry about the landmarks. I can do it under visual guidance. I stick in the needle and a gush of fluid comes out. I do chest compressions. The cardiac monitor shows a pulse. The vitals are coming back though his condition remains perilous.

"Oh my God," the nurse says.

"You're on fire," Dr. Richards congratulates me.

I blush and try not to get pumped up. I know I am not an exemplary clinician. I have a secret and I want to keep it that way.

I get aside. The intensivist and the ICU team

are here. They do the echocardiogram and get ready to transfer the patient to the ICU.

I get a pat on the back from the ER team. Dr. Richards orders free coffee for the entire team and I get a bonus donut as well.

I'm enjoying the black coffee and the chocolate donut. A sugar high. A nursing student comes and sits next to me at the central station. The name tag says, Mindy.

"Great job in saving the man in the resuscitation room."

"Thank you. I got lucky I guess."

"That man is lucky. We need doctors like you."

"Oh please."

"Do you want to go for breakfast after the shift?"

I'm taken aback. I admire her confidence. I'm flattered at being asked out. It's not dinner, but breakfast is not bad for a start. Hold on. I have a girlfriend. I can't cheat on her. I don't even know if Mindy is pretty. Without the skin, everyone looks the same. We're all wired that way.

My testosterone level is staying flat. I have a girlfriend which is an obstacle. The bigger obstacle is the predicament I'm in. My life is getting exponentially complicated. I must keep my sensual desires in check.

"Thanks for the offer but it may not be possible today as I'm flying back home." It's a polite no.

"Where is home?"

"Toronto, and you?"

"Home is right here. I need to get going. See you later. Let me know when you're free. You know where to find me."

She smiles and waves at me. I don't know if it's genuine. I smile back. Mine is fake.

I had a rollercoaster ride today. I experienced the energy of the roaring 20s, the hopelessness of the Great Depression, the exuberance of the dot com bubble, and the frustration of the financial collapse, all in a span of a few hours. The average of all these emotions is exhaustion. I sign out of the ER shift and head out to my apartment for a well-deserved sleep.

I walk to my apartment. It's early morning, the sun has not arisen yet. The roads are empty. I like it that way, fewer distractions but more danger. I could get mugged, but the probability is low. It's dawn. Criminals are sound asleep. They don't attack you at five in the morning. I climb the stairs to my apartment. My apartment is on the third floor, but I feel like I am climbing a mountain. My body has no energy left. I open the door, see the bed, and jump right at it.

CHAPTER 11

The sound of an alarm is the most annoying thing in the world. It's self-inflicted torture. Its shrill tone is shaking my eardrum. I feel like throwing away my smartphone. I don't do that obviously. It's my lifeline and it costs a lot of money.

Doing activities of daily living has become weird. I do nature's call with my eyes closed. Taking a shower seems redundant. I was never a fan of taking daily showers but since my skin is invisible now, I don't see the point of it at all. I have perfumes to take care of any odour. I take a shower, nevertheless. Habits die hard.

Breakfast is a mundane affair. There's nothing much to choose from. The fridge has milk, bread, jam, and a bowl of soup. It's bachelor life for you. Today's gourmet breakfast is stale chicken soup. It's two days old. I smell it, and it should be OK. I warm it up in the microwave hoping that some bacteria would die in the process.

I take a sip and squish it to feel the texture and the taste. It's salty. I don't remember it being that salty yesterday. Maybe the time has altered its taste. I continue chewing. Something is not right. I have never tasted something like this before. It's not a good taste. It's yucky. I use a finger to wipe out the secretions from my mouth. To my horror, it's blood. I run to the washroom. I spit in the sink. It's all blood. I rinse my mouth thoroughly. I checked my mouth to know the source of the bleeding. I don't see anything wrong. My gums and tongue look healthy. There is only one explanation, the chicken soup has turned into blood in my mouth. Don't ask me how, I am still trying to figure it out.

What the heck? Am I going to be a vegetarian now? I can live with that, but this paranormal stuff has a mind of its own. I drink milk, one step at a time. I keep checking for any blood. There is none. Good. At least I can have dairy. I check fruits as well. When I say fruits, I have only one banana. I eat it without noticing any blood.

I don't have the courage to try chicken soup again. It goes in the dustbin. To the environmental zealots out there, I do have an organics bin. I need to be careful with what I eat. It's true most of the time, but the stakes are much higher now. What we eat defines who we are.

I'm a bit scared after this experience. When you are scared, what comes to your mind? God, isn't it. Not all of you think of the Almighty but a fair number do I imagine. I must pay a visit to

His Holiness. There's a church nearby. I'm not a Christian but there's no ban on part-time believers in the church.

The church is one block away. It's at the intersection of Church Street and King Street. I brisk walk. I'm gasping for air. I slow down. I don't think I'll see a line up in front of the church. It's not Saint Peter's Basilica. It's a church with a nice cathedral but it's not imposing and it's not a major tourist attraction. I'm doing a walk-in visit. God doesn't keep an appointment list. I hope I'm right.

The door of the church is open. There is no lineup. There's not a living soul outside the premises. I take slow steps. I'm anticipating some reaction from my body. If I'm under some supernatural or paranormal influence, surely God can take care of it. That's the hypothesis. I have seen it in movies and some of them are based on real-life experiences.

Maybe some low bass voice will come from inside me. My eyeballs will turn all white. I'll start crawling backwards. Something like that. That's what happens in a possession.

I'm at the church door without an incident. Maybe something will happen as I enter the church. I take a deep breath as I take my first step inside the church. Nothing. The first thing I see is a big donation box. I have cash. I always keep cash. My credit score is fine, but you don't want to rely on digital currency all the time.

I take out a toonie, but I stop. Don't be

cheap man! I have my life on the line and all I could come up with is a toonie. Shameful. I have a twenty and a hundred-dollar bill. I contemplate. I put in the twenty-dollar bill. If I don't get what I want, I won't be disappointed with God. You may say charity should be string free. That's naive. God incentivizes good deeds. One good deed is all I need. I can now pray with good moral conviction.

I bow down and close my eyes. Nothing. My heart is beating fast. I have a laundry list of things to ask from the Almighty. I sprint through my prayer. It's anticlimactic. Why didn't anything happen? Maybe there is nothing paranormal going on here. Maybe ghosts are so used to praying that they're getting immune to it. Sort of like bugs which are getting resistant to antibiotics.

I see the priest. I see other worshippers. I see all their organs. That's disappointing. I see a worshipper with multiple metastases in his brain engaging in an extra-long prayer. He would be disappointed soon.

Maybe I'm not a true believer. Whatever may be the case, this visit has been a dud. But that's not true. Negative findings are also suggestive. A scientific approach may bode well. It's worth a try.

CHAPTER 12

It's advisable to stay in one's area of competence. Religion is not part of my core competence. The visit to the holy place was somewhat disappointing. I must do what I know best, treat it like a symptom and follow the algorithm. An eye checkup is in order.

Google map shows the nearest optometrist. It's half a block away in a strip mall. They take walk-ins. That's good. More walking to do but that's good for health.

I cover one eye to see if there is any discrepancy in the vision. There is none. I am finding new things with my newly discovered x-ray vision. Not only can I see internal human organs, but I can also visualize the outline of metal, plastic, and glass objects. That pretty much covers most of the things we use.

I can see the metallic rod in the leg of a passerby. The guy still limps. Job not done well by the orthopod.

I can see a tall woman walking toward me.

She has a big handbag, as big as a backpack. I can see inside. It's a designer handbag with a gold-plated strap. There are medicine bottles inside, and plastic make-up stuff. There's a knife inside. A Swiss knife? What's she up to? Maybe the knife is for self-protection.

She's walking fast despite wearing high heels. She's walking as if she's on a ramp. Her long and untied hair tell me the direction of the wind. She's wearing a black pantsuit. A bank employee? A serial killer? Both? Come on Sherlock Holmes, give up.

She's coming closer. We have eye contact. She stares at me like a cop. It's uncomfortable. I look away. She's strong. She passes by me. I don't look back at her. I should mind my own business.

I see a bunch of construction guys. They're smoking on the sidewalk. Two of them already have a beginning of emphysema. It's their life. If they want to die young, so be it. One guy has a handgun in his pocket. Carrying a handgun in Canada! How dare he? I know it's Alberta but still. I pause. Oh, it's a lighter. That makes sense. I smile at them. They don't.

I enter the optometrist's office. There are no patients waiting. The secretary asks me the reason for my visit. Of course, I don't tell her the truth. Routine exam.

She gives me a paper to fill out. It's quite intrusive. It has all kinds of questions about my heart and bowels. Why? If I have hemorrhoids, why do they need to find out? Maybe it is copy-pasted from a website. Not applicable is easy enough to write.

I'm taken to a dark room. The secretary instructs me to put my chin on an instrument pad. I'm told to press a button whenever I see flashes of light. My field of vision is being mapped. A gush of air is blasted onto my eyes to measure the eyeball pressure. A photo is taken of my retina. I read Snellen's chart. I have a 20/20 vision.

"Doctor will be in shortly." The secretary takes me to another room. I sit on a chair that resembles a dentist's chair.

The doctor arrives. He's wearing thick prescription glasses. That's confidence inspiring. Laser eye surgery ads are all over the office. I wonder why the good doctor didn't put himself under the laser.

Dr. Sharpe stares at my reports. He clicks on the computer and turns his neck to analyze the images. Oh, oh! Did he see something sinister? Does he know my secret?

"The images are over-saturated. I'm unable to make any diagnostic impression. We may have to repeat them," Dr. Sharpe says.

"No worries."

He didn't introduce himself. Neither did I. I like it that way.

I have another round of scans. The doctor still scratches his head.

"The images are no good. I apologize. There's

something wrong with the equipment." Dr. Sharpe keeps a poker face. He's worried. A big repair bill is no laughing matter.

"I hope it's your equipment doc if you don't mind me saying it."

"I understand. Don't worry, we have insurance. I won't charge you for the visit today. But we can still salvage the situation. I'll use the ophthalmoscope. You would need eye drops to dilate the pupils. Your vision may be blurry for a few hours. Don't drive."

"I won't."

He puts eye drops in my eyes. I wait five minutes. He comes closer to me. He steadies my head with his big hands. Dr. Sharpe is a huge guy. He could be a bouncer at a nightclub. Maybe he was.

His nose is almost touching mine. I can smell his breath. I hold mine. He rotates the ophthalmoscope. He snaps back. He takes off his glasses. He rubs his eyes. Doesn't say a word.

"Are you OK doc?"

He nods without saying a word. He takes a deep breath. He's ready for another try. Same result. He steps back. He closes his eyes for a few seconds and slowly opens them.

I'm alarmed. Wouldn't you?

"What's up doc?"

"I'm not sure. I can't see anything through the ophthalmoscope. It's like looking at bright light. I get blindsided. I think the ophthalmoscope is fine. I don't know how to explain this. I'm at a loss."

"Now what?" I am worried but relieved at the same time, at least my secret is safe.

"I'm going to refer you to an ophthalmologist."

"How long is the wait time?"

"Not long. Maybe six months."

"Great." Of course, it's not great, it's pathetic but that's the reality of current wait times in Canadian healthcare.

"I know the wait time is not ideal but it's not an emergency. I can't push for a sooner appointment."

"I'm here for only two weeks. I'm from Toronto."

"In that case, I would advise that you contact your family doctor or a local optometrist to do another referral in Ontario. Maybe the wait times are a bit better over there. I'll give you a copy of my consult note. Good luck."

I get a handwritten note. It's barely legible. The working diagnosis is to rule out retinal pathology. The diagnosis is legible because it's capitalized.

I take one step forwards and one step backward. I am still in the dark even though I can see everything clearly. I'm learning something new at every step of the way, but it only results in more questions than answers.

CHAPTER 13

I have a flight to catch today. Part of the weekend is already gone but I still got to go. Dad wants me to attend a function. It's not a family get-together. I have a suspicion it's some political event. He wants me to make contacts with the rich and the powerful. That's how you get ahead. He is sponsoring the trip. So, what's to complain about.

I'm late in checking in for the flight. All the good seats are gone. I don't want the middle seat. I do get a window seat but way back on the plane. 29 D is my seat. I have no checked bags. I'm going home, everything is there. It should cut my check-in time at the airport. We shall see.

The taxi arrives on time. That's a good start. The driver is South Asian which means he's going to explore my roots. I can bet on that. He's wearing a navy-blue turban. He has a trimmed beard. He's a heavy guy. He has put the driver's seat all the way back to create room for his heavy bottom. His protruding belly is preventing his tight half sleeve shirt to be tucked into the trousers. He doesn't care about his looks. An admirable quality.

"Where are you from?" I was expecting this question. He asks it five minutes into the journey.

"Toronto." I keep it short.

"I mean originally, which country, India or Pakistan?" He's not giving up.

"I am Canadian-born."

"I can tell that from your accent. What about your parents?"

"They came from India."

"Which part?" The excitement is palpable in his voice.

"Punjab."

"Where in Punjab?"

"Amritsar."

"Guru ka ghar (the home of the Guru)."

"Yes." Please no more questions but I doubt he will stop now.

"Where in Amritsar?"

"Some colony, I don't remember. It's been a while since I've been there.

"Do you speak Punjabi?"

"I can understand it, but speaking is a stretch."

"It's good to know your mother tongue. I have made sure my children know Punjabi well."

"Good for you and good for them."

"You guys have it easy. When I came to Canada in 1984, things were difficult here, but they were horrible in Punjab. There was a struggle every step of the way." He doesn't stop there. He tells me where he was born, how wonderful his childhood was, the simplicity of life back then, and the exchange rate of the Indian rupee to the Canadian dollar in those times.

He finishes his autobiography with the cliché, "You can take me out of Punjab, but you can't take Punjab out of me."

I smile. I don't want to encourage him. It's distracted driving. It's dangerous. He keeps turning back when talking to me.

"Be careful," I stress upon him to keep his eyes on the road.

"Don't worry brother, I can drive with my eyes closed." I don't like the overconfident types. I don't like that he called me brother either. He's of my dad's age but wants to be a millennial.

He points to a Punjabi restaurant on the road," If you want authentic Indian sweets, try here."

"Thanks," I say in the hope he will shut up.

I can't help but notice that his organs are covered with a layer of fat. They give out a golden hue. I get a side view of the heart. The right coronary artery is clogged. Oh boy. If his left one is of the same caliber, then he doesn't have much time left in this world.

I feel sorry for him. Should I tell him that he's one steak away from a heart attack? How should I frame it so that it comes out naturally?

"Punjabis need to be careful. We are at high risk for diabetes and heart disease. We need to be careful about what we eat."

"If Punjabis start eating only salads, then that's the end of our way of life. Doctors push tests, drug companies push pills, and you know what I do?"

It's a rhetorical question. I don't take the bait. I keep quiet.

"I'll tell you. I push back." There's a glee in his eyes.

Smarty-pants. I respond in kind," You should push dumbbells, not science."

"Ha, ha. Let's agree to disagree. Do you study here?"

I'm glad to change the topic. Another intrusive question. I'll give him the information in snippets.

"Yes, I do. The University of Calgary."

"It's expensive, man. Costs thousands of dollars. What are you studying? Engineering?"

A closed-ended question. I should say yes and move on but lying is cumbersome. One lie leads to another.

"I study medicine."

"Wow. You must be intelligent. You're going to be a doctor. Doctors mint money. Work hard now and keep counting the dollars for the rest of your life."

"It's not that simple. Life is stressful in medicine. Money is not everything."

"They say money can't buy happiness. That's a lie. If I ever win a jackpot, my happiness will know no bounds."

I nod. There's no point in having an argument. I want to arrive alive at the airport. I have set his expectations high. How much should I tip? He's probably going to die in a couple of years. I better be generous. Money gives him happiness. Let's give him some.

I have a suspicion that he's taking me on a longer route to the airport.

"Airport seems quite far away."

He gets the point. "I'm picking the sideroads. The highway gets busy. There's construction going on. The route may be longer, but we will reach on time."

Whether I trust him or not, I am stuck with him. I started three hours before the flight time. No need to panic yet.

We arrive at the airport. The meter shows forty-five dollars. I have a fifty-dollar bill. That's all he will get. I hand him the note.

"Don't worry about the change."

He's not impressed. He doesn't say thank you, but I say good luck to him.

CHAPTER 14

The airport is busy. It always is. Kids are off from school. Parents are desperate to get out. It's time to spend all those savings. They have packed almost half of their belongings. Trolleys are overloaded and check-in bag lines run forever. I'm glad to skip Those lines. I check the departure board; my flight is on time.

The screening lines are moving at a snail's pace. People are carrying so much stuff for the holidays and they'll buy even more stuff on vacation. Bunch of hoarders. Kids are getting restless. Adult tempers are flaring. I choose a line with no kids, maybe it will move faster.

The guy in front has a big carry-on bag. An entire shaving kit is stored inside. There are shaving blades and sharp scissors. He would need secondary screening. He will slow us all down. I can't change the line now, it's too late. He's wearing a strong perfume, but his clothes look shabby. His T-shirt is off-white from lack of laundry. Maybe that's why he wears a strong perfume.

I am number three in line. The first guy in line is immaculately dressed. He's wearing a full sleeve shirt, pleated trousers, and dress shoes. An office worker. A business trip perhaps. He's wearing glasses to cement his studious look. He's nicely trimmed. He's wearing a Rolex Daytona. Guy has money. His abdomen is flat as a board. I'm jealous. He's five feet ten inches, one inch smaller than me. I'm happy about that.

He has a patch on his left arm. Why? A nitrate patch? He's a young guy, probably in his 30s, he can't have angina. My bad. Maybe a nicotine patch. Good for him. He is breaking a bad habit. The sooner the better. He is young and if he wants to live longer, he must give up smoking. I admire his spirit.

Something doesn't make sense. I look closely. I turn my head to look from different angles. It's not just one patch, I can count thirty. He's also wearing patches on both thighs; again, multiple packages are packed inside thin plastic covering. It's all under the skin.

There's something fishy going on. Drugs. Fentanyl probably. A drug dealer. A cunning one at that. But today won't end well for him. He will get caught. A pat-down would nail him.

He breezes through the screening. No beep from the metal detectors obviously. No secondary screening. No pat-down. And there he goes. Typical.

The guy with the shaving kit is called

for secondary screening. It was inevitable. He deserves it.

It's my turn. I take a deep breath and walk through the metal detector. There is a beep. I get the pat-down treatment. I remove my shoes. I turn around for the agents to admire my body at different angles. Of course, they can't find anything incriminating. There's a coin in my back pocket. It was enough to put me through the humiliation. I know I'm not carrying anything illegal but getting beeped at and patted down is still unnerving.

They must let me go but I'm not going to let them go. They let away a drug dealer and patted me down for a coin in my pocket. I'm angry. It's time to show them the mirror. It's my civic duty too. Drugs harm everyone and criminals are a menace to society. It's a risky move though. I want to keep my identity under the wraps. Who wants to mess with the underworld?

I give the description of the offending person. He's still visible at a distance. I point straight at him. I tell them to check underneath the skin on his arms and thighs. It's beyond the pay grade of the security guy. He calls for backup. I request anonymity. I don't want any reward. I cherish my safety. Life is precious and no amount of money can bring a life back.

"No problem but if you are lying then you are in trouble," the security guy warns me.

"That's fair."

The security guy wants to see my boarding pass in case I need to be summoned. I oblige. I'm not playing a prank. It's dead serious and I am glad he takes it seriously as well.

I walk briskly to get away from the screening area. I watch at a distance that the drug dealer is taken for questioning into a room. He's accompanied by five police officers and a police dog. Rest is not my problem. I will read it in the news.

CHAPTER 15

I'm at the gate. There is no seat in the waiting area. It's a full flight. The crew are pleading for everyone to be patient. They are irritated by seeing so many carry-ons. I scan the carry-ons. I am not paid to do it. I do it because I can. Nothing suspicious. Clothes, perfumes, toys, including adult toys, and condoms, lots of them. It's good. People want to be safe and safe sex is always better.

The pilots pass by. I scan them from top to bottom. Their health is critical to my survival. The older pilot has the beginnings of an enlarged prostate, not a biggie. The younger one has nodules in the thyroid, probably an incidental finding and not relevant for this flight. I sign off on their health. Not that I could do anything about it if something was wrong except not to fly.

That's also the way with the weather. There's a strong thunderstorm watch, not a warning yet. It may be a bumpy ride. I hate turbulence. It's in my destiny to be anxious but I can't stop living because of my fears.

The boarding starts. I'm at the end of the line. I find my seat. The middle and the aisle seats are already occupied. 29D is waiting for my bottom to rest on it. In the middle seat, there is a teenager. The confidence interval for her age is between 16 to 21 years. The vitality of the skin aids in age recognition. But I can look for other clues like jeans that are ripped in multiple places and T-shirt that's skin-tight and with provocative slogans. The lipstick is bright, and the perfume is strong. The aisle seat is occupied by an old lady. I can't see her wrinkles, but I can see her hunched back from osteoporosis. It's a good enough clue. Her small handbag is full of medicines. She's obsessed with her health. The teenager is obsessed with her looks, and I'm obsessed with finding faults in others.

There's no space to put carry-on luggage in the overhead compartment. My carry-on goes under the seat. The ladies make way for me to pass through. I make myself comfortable and put the seat belt on. The smartphone is set to airport mode. I make sure there is a sickness bag in the front seat pocket in case I vomit, which is a distinct possibility. I read the onboard instructions carefully and glance at the lifejacket under the seat. The probability is infinitely small that it will ever be used but you never know.

The pre departure checks are completed. I watch the pre-flight video with all my attention. The teenager is listening to music. She has earbuds for that. She's all prepared. Typical casualness. The old lady is still figuring out how the inflight entertainment works.

The take-off is smooth. No signs of thunderstorms. The view from the window seat is mesmerizing. The Rockies are as beautiful from above as they are from the ground.

The old lady asks for help from the teen in figuring out the entertainment console. The teen knows it all. She's sharp.

"I haven't flown in ten years," the old lady says.

"Really," the teenager reacts. The lady has been living under the rock.

"Magical that we can fly in the air above the clouds but it's expensive and tiring."

"Yup."

"I'm going to meet my grandson. He's one month old. My daughter lives in Toronto."

"Congrats, you must be excited."

"Thanks. Yes, I am."

"Your first grandchild?"

"No, it's my fourth but the excitement never wanes."

"True."

"And what about you? Are you also going to see your family?"

"No, I am starting university in September. I'm going to U of T. It's hard to find a place in downtown Toronto. It's better to start early."

"Your parents must be proud."

"I don't know about that."

"I bet they are. What are you going to study?"

"Biomedical engineering."

"What's that?"

"It involves designing medical devices. I'll see if I like it."

"Good luck."

"Thanks."

The in-flight service has started. Nothing is free. Airlines have razor-thin margins. They want to squeeze every penny out of you. The old lady asks for a glass of wine.

"Do you want to have one?" She asks the teen.

"No, I don't want to pay."

"Don't worry, it's on me. You're such a sweet girl."

"Thank you so much. In that case, I'll have one."

They get a glass of local wine. Nothing fancy. I am not even asked. I was not expecting it either.

I am the silent bystander. They are talking non-stop. It's hard not to pay attention.

I order orange juice and chips. I keep it simple. The ladies get chips and salad.

"Cheers!" They take the first sip of wine.

Obviously, I won't join them. I pretend to be disinterested. I glance at them at an angle. Something is pulsating in the teen's belly. Her heart? It can't be. The location is wrong. The pulsation is coming from way down.

I drop the chips bag so I can pick it up from the floor. I get down to pick up the bag and get a clear view of her abdomen. The pulsation is coming from inside her pelvis. There's a tiny round mass that is rapidly pulsating. Oh my God! It's early pregnancy.

Does she know? Probably not. How dare she drink alcohol? No amount of alcohol is safe. What should I do? I can't tell her. Not directly. She would freak out. And how do I convince her that she is pregnant? Would she believe me? I don't have answers to these questions yet.

Desperate times call for desperate measures. I will torpedo her drink. I sneeze; it's a fake sneeze but my elbow hits her drink, and it pills. I take care that the drink spills away from her and towards the front chair. Spilling the drink directly on her would have been disastrous. I may be perceived as mischievous or downright dirty. It works, the drink is spilled, and no one gets the splash. Job done.

"I'm so sorry. I didn't mean to spill your drink." I try to show remorse. I took acting lessons once. They obviously helped.

"It's alright," she says with a fake smile. She is not happy but she's not angry either. I'll take that.

"I'll buy you another drink."

"No, that's alright."

"Please allow me to. Otherwise, I will not forgive myself."

I called the flight attendant. "Can I order another drink?"

"Sure."

"Do you have orange juice?"

"Yes, we do."

"Is orange juice OK for you? I ask the teen. I have put her in a dilemma. A close-ended question. Please say yes.

"Yes, that's fine."

Mission accomplished but not quite. I may have torpedoed her drink, but I can't stop her from drinking once she's off the plane. She needs to be told the truth. But how?

"Do you know the health benefits of wine? I ask the ladies.

They look surprised.

"I don't know," the teen says with an attitude.

"I did a paper on the risks and benefits of wine in the first year of medical school." I boast of my academic credentials. Of course, I am lying.

"Oh," the teen pretends to be interested.

"You did," the old lady sounds more authentic.

I quote some studies and the modest benefits of wine on various body organs. I keep it deliberately vague. I had to because I'm no expert in wine. But I have become an expert in lying.

"Oh yeah," another non-enthusiastic

response from the teen.

"And there are harms of course. Pregnancy being one. Fetal alcohol syndrome is a tragic result. No amount of alcohol is safe in pregnancy."

"Of course," the old lady agrees.

"The sad part is that many women don't even realize that they could be pregnant. They keep drinking. It's especially true if dates get mixed up."

I could see the teen's heart beating fast. The sympathetic system has been activated. I have instilled fear in her. Maybe she'll do a home pregnancy test.

"Sorry for the unsolicited medical talk." It's time for me to wrap up.

"No worries," the old lady says.

The teen stays silent. She's probably contemplating the dreaded scenario of an unwanted pregnancy. Women's choice is paramount in Canada. But still making that choice is painful.

I close my eyes. No more sightseeing. No more diagnostic conclusions. I begin the countdown for the flight to end. I count from one to a hundred and backward. It keeps me busy.

CHAPTER 16

Captain has activated the seatbelt sign. This announcement always gives me chills. I know this is routine in preparation for the arrival but still, every bump makes my heart skip. The landing is smooth. Thank God. Good job Captain. The ladies share pleasantries. I am excluded again. Landing a plane is no guarantee of an on-time arrival. It takes further 30 minutes for the plane to arrive at the gate, crisscrossing through the maze of airport roads. I am the last to disembark. It takes time for the passengers to get all their belongings and their kids. No kid should be left behind. I am on the ground. I am just happy about that.

People are running to get out of the airport. It's not so easy. Check-in baggage takes its own sweet time. I have no such troubles.

No taxi for me today. I'll take the public transit. There is a direct train from the airport to downtown Toronto. It's fast and efficient. There were not many passengers inside. I have the entire row to myself. No neighbors. Like real estate, having no neighbors is an asset on the train. I have learned this from my dad. He always buys properties with no rear neighbors. Apparently, it has universal appeal.

I reach downtown Toronto. I study here but don't live here. Too expensive. I live in the West End near High Park. It's cheaper, better, and safer in my opinion. I must change two more subway trains to reach my destination. I have a monthly pass. It's the cheaper option. There is a theme here. I'm not thrilled about spending money. It's opposite to my dad, who often goes on shopping sprees. It boosts his ego, but no amount of money can quench the thirst of desire. I too like good quality clothes but only when they are on sale. The margin on clothes is ginormous. But on sale doesn't mean hoarding clothes. 2-3 pairs of jeans last me a decade.

I reach the apartment building. I have a bachelor's apartment. It's one big hall. No bedroom, no lobby, and one washroom. Plenty for me. There's no carpet. It's all vinyl. Easy to clean. My apartment has a city view, basically urban sprawl. The lake view is too expensive. I can just walk there for the view. Why pay hundreds of dollars for that?

I open the door of my apartment. It smells the same as I left it, damp and dusty. The vinyl floor hides all the dust. The bedding is beige as well. Ignorance is bliss in this case. If I can't see dust, then it's clean for me. If I ever work in a hospital, I'm never going to oversee infection control. My brown skin also hides dust well. Now since my skin is invisible, I don't even have to worry about that either unless someone points it out to me.

Speaking of that, the honor of pointing out mistakes in me goes to my girlfriend. My dad comes close second. My girlfriend's name is Sawaal. She's good at a lot of things but first and foremost is her ability to ask questions. No wonder she's studying law. It's a long story about how she ended up in law but that's what novels are for. I'll keep it short.

We met in the first year of medical school. The first thing she asked me was my name, but I didn't have to ask hers. She's not shy. She is assertive. She's smart. She's petite. Fifty-five kilos to be precise. She is five feet three inches tall. Beauty is subjective but let's say she's not model material. I'm OK with that. She's caring and that's what matters. She's strong and can stand up to authority. She didn't like medical school and decided to go into law. We had a fight, more a series of arguments and she won, the sign of a good lawyer. She's happy in law school, and I'm happy in medical school, that makes us both happy.

Lawyers earn less than doctors. She would argue against this assertion. She tells me to wait and see. She wants to climb the corporate law ladder. She is ambitious. Bay Street is waiting for her.

My parents have mixed feelings for her.

Mom's first reaction was that she was not as tall as her. It's not a competition for God's sake. She was thinking about future offspring. She's not a geneticist, genes can skip generations. Sawaal's parents are blue-collared. Her older sister is a pharmacist. A younger brother is in high school. My parents were not thrilled about having blue collared in-laws. They consoled themselves that at least the girl would be wearing a white coat. I didn't tell them for a while that she quit medical school. Once she got good grades in law school, I broke the news. They went into grief. It took them quite a while to reach the acceptance stage. Her co-op with a top Bay Street law firm made it possible.

Whenever I talk about her with my parents, which is not a lot, the only question they have is, if she is happy in law school? They don't want another surprise career change. If she does that, I may have to find a new girlfriend.

I text her that I am home. She replies right back. I like her promptness. She'll be there at my apartment in thirty minutes.

I'm nervous. I don't know what to tell her. I don't know how she will take it. I'm not ready to tell the truth. We are not married. They are no vows to uphold. All it takes to end a relationship is a text message. She could take it the wrong way, maybe I'm delusional or worse, that I do drugs. She's a lawyer, she would go for the most rational explanation.

I will lie to her. People have lied to loved ones

before. I'm no exception.

She has keys to my apartment. She offered hers as well which I gladly passed. If anything were to go missing in her apartment, I would have been indicted. She doesn't come unannounced. She is respectful of my privacy.

The bell rings. She's there. I take a deep breath.

"Hi," she smiles.

"Hi," I want to gasp but hold back. I'm getting used to seeing people without any skin but she's my girlfriend for heaven's sake. I'm not dating her for her looks but the thought of making it out with a cadaver face gives me creeps.

"How are you doing?"

"I'm alright." I lie, my heart is beating fast, but she can't see that. I can.

"Good. How was your flight?"

"Smooth."

Her handbag is heavy. I take it from her. I have learned to be chivalrous. It's negative reinforcement. If I forget, she will remind me. The bag is full of legal papers, not make-up. My kind of girl.

She puts her arms around me.

"Did you miss me?"

"Of course, I did."

Is it a lie? Of course, it is.

She comes forward to kiss me. I can't refuse. I close my eyes. I don't want to have a close-up view of her tonsils and glands on her tongue. I stiffen my lips. I peck on her cheek.

"Are you alright?"

"I haven't brushed my teeth. I don't want you to smell my bad breath." You see, her questions never stop.

"Did you have dinner yet?"

"No, I didn't."

"Should we order fried chicken?"

No! I want to scream.

"I'm not that hungry. I'll have fruit salad. Unless you want to order."

"OK, I'll have the same."

I open the fridge and take out the ready-to-eat salad bowl. I remove the plastic covering. I use the plastic fork. Minimal work. I stress out whenever I eat in front of her. She hears all kinds of noises coming from my mouth. She hates it. Come on, I need to chew. I still do it but in slow motion. But that takes the fun out of eating.

"How has your experience been in Calgary?"

"Good."

"That's all. You're probably tired. But I want to hear everything that happened up there. You didn't call me for two days. I thought you were probably busy. I'll forgive you this time."

"Yeah! I was."

Fewer words, less trouble, minimal lying. She's a lawyer. She picks through each sentence.

"Do you want anything to drink?" It's a rhetorical question. I don't have anything in the fridge except water.

"What are the options?"

"Water, tap or filtered. I still have to do grocery shopping."

"Filtered obviously."

She stands up and pulls her top off.

"Hold on," I say. "I'm not in the mood. I have a bad headache."

"Listen to yourself. I'm not trying to jump on you. I did some shopping today. I want to show what I bought."

"My bad. I'm sorry. Sure, go ahead." I don't hesitate to apologize. It saves me grief every time.

She's a fan of Indian kurtas. She bought five of them. They all look the same to me.

"They all look good on you." She's not done. I know a guessing game is about to start.

"Can you guess how much these are?"

"Hundred dollars?"

"Only forty-five. Bargain, isn't it?"

"Yes, it is."

The smile on her face is worth more than a hundred dollars. I play along. I overshoot. I know she buys on sale. But validating someone's choice always pays off.

She's ready to leave. We don't sleep together. It's not due to some moral dilemma. I have a single bed and I toss and turn all night.

She waves goodbye with a flying kiss. I reciprocate. I'm glad she is gone. I love her but I need to be left alone today.

CHAPTER 17

The next morning, I am awake early. With adrenaline overflowing in my blood, who wants to sleep? The first order of business is to check the news. I am eager to know what happened to the guy who was allegedly smuggling drugs. I search for Calgary airport and in the news section, there are lots of hits on the person who was nabbed by authorities trying to smuggle hundreds of fentanyl patches hiding under the skin. It's a big heist. The offender is known by the name Sniffer in organized crime circles. He is the brother of the kingpin of organized crime in Calgary, a guy known as the Injector. I feel edgy. Who wouldn't be? I have made enemies with organized crime. I have sent the brother of the Drug Lord to prison. Not good for my health and well-being. I wish to remain anonymous to them. It's out of my hands. Not knowing is suffering.

I'm heading home. My parents live in Oakville. They live on the waterfront, in an enclave of multi-million-dollar homes. You must be thinking what a spoiled brat, born with a silver spoon. But remember my parents are doctors, and my mom is a health freak. I got fed with all kinds of vitamins and minerals with the same silver spoon. Let me tell you, those medicines suck even if you get them with a silver spoon or a plastic one.

I get the car ready. I have one parking spot in the underground parking. I have an old Honda Civic, cheap, and reliable, and suits my needs. I start at 8:00 AM sharp. It's critical to plan the trip out of downtown Toronto. Traffic jams happen suddenly. A stalled vehicle is enough to cause traffic chaos.

I'm out of the downtown core without encountering any delays. QEW is wide open. I respect the speed limit, in spirit and in practice. Most others don't. I annoy other drivers. They tailgate me. I move to the right lane. Even the dump trucks find me annoying. They overtake me. They give me angry looks as they pass by. A nervous driver. One guy gives me the finger as well. I'm used to it. It's the price to pay for doing the right thing.

The road is turning downhill. It's a steep incline. I take my foot off the accelerator. Gravity will push the car. My phone rings. Of course, I'm on Bluetooth. It's mom.

"Have you started?"

"Yes, I'm on my way."

"What time will you reach?"

"In about forty minutes give and take."

"OK, see you then."

Typical. She still babies me.

I check the speedometer. I'm going at 110 km/hr in an 80 km/hr zone. I panic. I apply the brakes. I underestimated the gravity of the situation. Maybe I'll get away.

The police cruiser is behind me. Oh, please no flashing lights. It's wishful thinking. The cop puts the flashers on. I pull over and put the hazard lights on. I'm busted.

I blame the cop, zealous. I blame my mom, overbearing. I blame myself, stupid. My stellar driving record is going to be blemished.

The cop comes out of the car. He's taking a leisurely stride. He is heavy. He's wearing sunglasses, part of a cop uniform. Makes them look cool and intimidating. It's a cloudy day but that doesn't matter to the cop.

"Do you know what speed you were driving at?" The cop's voice is clear and stern.

"Sorry, it was a steep slope. I didn't realize that." I keep my pitch low.

"That was not what I asked."

"95," I low ball.

"No Sir, you were going at 110."

"Sorry, but I was in the slow lane. People were passing right by me."

"That doesn't make what you did right."

"But the others were traveling even faster."

"Yeah, but you got caught."

"That's not fair."

"Of course, it is. I can only catch one culprit at a time. You are the fish that got caught."

"Is it possible that you can let me go this time?"

"Why?"

"I'm not a habitual speedster. I drive with care. It's my first and only mistake."

"I refuse to believe that. You were lucky that you didn't get caught earlier. But today is another day. Deal with it. There will be a fine and a few demerit points. You can challenge it in court but don't count on it. Please show me your driving license and insurance papers."

I hand over the papers. I'm well organized that way. The papers are in order. I had prepared for this eventuality. The guy is heartless even though his heart is big. The cardio-thoracic ratio is high. Probably has high blood pressure. Not a surprise. He spends a few minutes in the car. He's getting the ticket ready. My insurance will go up. I will cut back on take-out orders. I'm budgeting for an increase in future expenses.

"Here is the ticket. Be careful next time. Speed kills. You are young. I'm sure you don't want to die young. Driving is a privilege. Treat it that way. If you try hard, you can do it."

I'm annoyed. This ticket is unfair. I don't like his holier-than-thou attitude. He's probably in his 50s. He has plenty of grey hair. His lungs are overexpanded. Not a good thing. He likely has emphysema meaning he's a chronic smoker. His heart must push against the pressure coming from the lungs. Pulmonary hypertension. Not a good sign. I can smell smoke on him.

He has puffers and a pack of cigarettes in his pocket. Hypocrite.

"I'll keep that in mind, officer. I quit smoking years ago. Some people keep on smoking even though they know that their lungs are getting cooked. Their heart gets big, and they keep puffers in their pockets but still light a cigarette. Some habits die hard you know."

The cop keeps a poker face. His sweat glands are activated, and his heart rate has increased. He's spooked.

"You can go now." His voice is feeble. He has been shown the mirror. He deserves it. I don't say thank you. What's there to be thankful about? I'll pay the ticket. He'll pay the price for smoking. Hopefully, I have shaken him enough for him to let go of the unsuspecting drivers at the bottom of the hill.

CHAPTER 18

I'm at the gates. Yes, my parents live in a gated community. They pay $256 per month for the privilege. Chump change for a sound night sleep for them. I get buzzed in. Most homes are on one acre lots. The coveted ones face the waterfront and appreciate more than the others. That's what my dad thought when he bought the house. It was custom built. He overextended himself to buy the house. It meant he had to do plenty of colonoscopies to pay off the mortgage and that's what he did. He continues to plow through the colonoscopies even though the mortgage is paid off. He starts the scopes at 6:45 AM till 5:30 PM. He has single-handedly reduced the wait time for colon cancer screening in the city of Oakville. It's a privileged community and people are health conscious. They line up for their scopes.

Dad is a tall guy, six feet four inches to be exact. His hands are proportionately big. When he does a rectal exam, it's a mini scope. Probably painful. I'm not that tall. Damn genes. They skip generation sometimes. His hairline is receding. I hope the genes skip that trait as well otherwise it would be a bummer. He has an elongated face with crooked teeth. Not a looker.

But my mom is. She looks younger than her age. She is not tall, five feet four inches at most but her looks more than make up for the lack of height. She colors her hair. Makeup is top-notch. She wears ethnic clothes which are colorful and bright. She's a psychiatrist. Her bubbly personality helps those depressed and anxious patients.

If dad talks in dollar terms, mom talks in spiritual terms. She's into yoga and meditation. Dad plays golf and mom does asanas. It's a mismatch that works. Dad controls money and mom controls emotions. They have their fights. They make up. Give and take happens on both sides. They are still married and that's what matters to me.

I park the car in the garage. The house has a four-car garage. I don't ring the bell. I have the keys. The door is tall and sturdy. It's a fiberglass door. A surveillance camera welcomes you. Dad will get the notification that I am at the door.

The foyer has a high ceiling with a huge chandelier. It is sure to impress any guest. I have seen it many times and it still awes me. My only worry is that if any of the bulbs fuse, it would be a pain to replace.

I make it to the family room. Dad is reading the newspaper, probably going through analyst recommendations on stocks. He can tell you the stock price, market capitalization, and the YTD return on all the Dow components. Mom looks at Dad, shakes her head, and mumbles, "Money, money, money!"

"Hi Mom, hi Dad."

"Hi, Karan," Mom responds.

Dad only waves.

"Mom, you look pretty." I'm lying. I'm horrified to see her skinless face and internal organs. But I must still give a compliment. It's a compulsion. If I don't, she would make me say it. She's insecure about her looks. She cannot reconcile that she is getting old. She's proud of her looks, but like yesterday year's actress, she's holding onto the past more than the present.

"What about me?" Dad wants his validation too.

"You look dapper in your pyjamas."

"I got it on sale at Harry Rosen. Made in Italy."

"Great," I can smell snobbishness. No, it's his new perfume, also made in Italy or France.

"How did you find Alberta?" Mom inquires.

"Beautiful, clean, and conservative."

"Do you still want to work with dead people?" Dad can't help himself.

"Dead people don't complain, you know."

"Yeah, but dead people don't pay bills either."

"They don't need to pay. The Ministry of

Health will."

"And they take away 50% at the source. Salaries are for suckers."

"Salaries come with benefits."

"It's a fallacy. They don't make up for that ginormous tax bill that has to be prepaid."

"It's still worth it in my opinion."

"How's the girlfriend?" Dad doesn't say her name. Passive-aggressor-in-chief.

"She's fine. She's climbing the corporate ladder."

"Good for her. Hope she values money. Otherwise, you'll be stuck in social housing all your life."

"Come on Dad, condo living is not social housing. It's a good lifestyle. Minimal work, maximum luxury."

"Condos are oversized boxes with windows."

"If it is so then maybe we'll have some inheritance from you someday."

"Don't talk like that," Mom is superstitious.

"Sorry, Mom."

"Don't count on my money. You're not a crown prince who's waiting for the coronation."

"Let's change the topic. How's Nikki?" I ask Mom.

Nikki is my older sister. Dad's favorite. She's in the first year of ophthalmology residency at the University of Western Ontario. Bright, ambitious, and ruthless. Just like Dad.

"She is busy. First year of residency is brutal.

She came home on Friday for an hour or so. Go, go, go. That's her." Mom sympathizes with her.

"That's the cost of excellence. She knows what she wants. She wants to go into laser eye surgery. She'll rake millions." Dad is beaming with pride.

"You must be proud of her?" I ask Dad grudgingly.

"We are proud of you both," Mom interjects. She's thoughtful. That's what you expect of your mom.

"I have made tea for you. Have some."

"Thanks, Mom."

I give her thumbs up. I sit at the breakfast table. It's made of solid mahogany wood. Expensive but uncomfortable. She joins me. Dad is still busy going through the newspaper, looking into the latest stock recommendations. He's looking for a ten-bagger. He is a Peter Lynch fan.

"Dad loves you. Don't take everything that he says to heart. He means well." Mom says it with a calm voice.

I don't agree but I still nod.

CHAPTER 19

I've never been this uncomfortable in my life. Mom is sitting in front of me. I can see through her clothes. Seeing one's parents naked is not a pleasant sight. It's a different type of nakedness, without the skin. I glance at her breasts. I didn't want to, but I had to. There is a shiny nodule in her right breast. I can't ignore it. I feel sick. Is it cancerous?

She's in her 50s. The prime age for getting breast cancer. No family history but her family lived in India and breast screening was non-existence in those days. I need to take a good look at the nodule but staring at her breasts is awkward and downright creepy.

"Mom, please close your eyes."

"Why?"

"I think there is an eyelash on your face."

"Don't lose it."

She's superstitious. She believes that blowing an eyelash off your hand can grant you any wish. She gets this invaluable knowledge from her mom who has an encyclopedic knowledge of all things superstitious.

I have only a few seconds. I move forward and scan the nodule at different angles. It's smooth and there are no enlarged lymph nodes in the armpit. Good signs. I feel reassured but not quite. I'm not a trained radiologist. Breast imaging is its own subspeciality and I could be wrong.

She opens her eyes.

"Sorry, it was a mistake. There was no eyelash, just a speck of dust."

She is obviously disappointed. The wish that was not meant to be.

"How's your health?" I try to make an opening.

"I'm alright. Why do you ask?"

"You are in your 50s. You need to be on the top of cancer screening."

"Thanks for reminding me of my age. I am up to date with all the tests."

"When did you have your mammogram?"

"Last year."

"Was it OK?"

"Not exactly. There was one nodule. I got scared at first. I went for special views. It turned out to be benign."

"You didn't tell me that."

"I don't need to. These things happen."

"Which side was it?"

"I think it was on the right side towards the outer part."

It corresponds to the nodule I visualized. Thank God. It's unconscionable to think that your parents are going to die. One day they will, but not today, not tomorrow.

"Karan, get ready. We must leave in half an hour. I don't want to be late." Dad has given the orders. He means business.

"Where are we going?"

It's dinner. A donor event. The Premier of Alberta is coming. We need to support him. He deserves our support.

"We live in Ontario. Why bother with him?"

"He's a beacon of conservatism. He likes free capital but not free money. He deserves our dollars."

"But why should I have to go?"

"Because you need to move in high circles. Only then can you reach high places."

"You don't reach anywhere moving in a circle."

"Don't quibble with words."

"That's what politicians do. And you like politicians."

"True but you're not a politician. Let's not waste any more time."

I back off. I always do. I don't like confrontation. It's worse than humiliation.

I wear a black suit with a matching black tie. Dad wears a bow tie. Mom wears a western dress for a change. It's bright red. It will help us blend in with the crowd except our skin is a tad darker than the average political attendee.

Dad fires up his Bentley. When I save fires up, it whispers, quiet and sophisticated. The convention centre is twenty kilometers away. It's 7:30 PM already. The roads are still busy but not jammed.

It takes five minutes for us to find the parking spot. Dad is not annoyed. The event is a hit. More donors, the better. He parks it with the help of an automated parking assist. It's a perfect job.

"Be careful when you open the door."

Dad is not worried about denting other people's cars. He is more worried about keeping his Bentley scratch-free.

Mom is uncomfortable in high heels. But it makes her reach the shoulder length of Dad. It moderates the height discrepancy in them. It makes her happy.

The hall is full. We are escorted to our table. Our names are placed on the table. The table is close to the podium. Money grants access.

There is a three-course meal. Full range of drinks. No limit. We have paid for it. I am sure some will make up for the donated money by splurging on drinks.

Introductory speeches are cringe-worthy but short. The Premier of Alberta Mr. Green Oilfield arrives on the stage. A standing ovation is in order. Claps are deafening. A friendly crowd except for the media who are busy recording his every move and waiting for an embarrassing slip-up.

Mr. Oilfield is a chubby fellow. He smiles big. Why won't he? He is the darling of the right. He could be a stand-up comedian, but his smile is a deception. His speeches are loaded with anger, doomsday scenarios, and conspiracy theories. Premier killjoy, not that most politicians bring joy to people.

Dad is pumped up. Mom is indifferent. I suppress a yawn. I don't have much money, I don't have to worry about taxes, not yet anyway.

Mr. Oilfield is going on and on. I watch his every move. Nothing else to do. The guy's bladder is full. He had a couple of drinks before he came in. There is some dribbling of urine every time he shouts a slogan. Yuck. His prostate is big. Not a surprise for a guy in his 60s. I can see some irregularity in the prostate. Not good news. I don't have a clear view. I stand up and go to the side of the podium.

"Sit down!" Dad mumbles.

I ignore him. I pretend to take pictures of the man. No one stops me. I have a clear view of the prostate. There's a nodule in there. The capsule seems intact. Lymph nodes in the groin are also normal. Maybe prostate cancer, maybe not. Only a biopsy can tell. PSA may help.

I sit down. Dad gives me a dressing down. I have no trouble swallowing my pride. But I do have trouble swallowing the steak which is presented in front of me. I leave it as is.

"Why are you not eating the steak?" Typical Mom.

"I have gone vegetarian."

"Since when?"

"Since I went to Calgary."

"I'll buy you a whole bunch of multivitamins. Don't lose out on proteins." Mom is going to drown me with health products. My taste buds would get toasted. I see trouble.

I start eating the salad. It's bland but I have no choice. Dessert is the saving grace. I never miss out on a creamy chocolate cake. To hell with calories and sugar content.

It's time for pictures and handshakes with the Premier. Donors want the personal touch. They are not here to just listen to speeches.

The Premier comes to our table. We are at the front and first in line. I'm in two minds. Should I tell the guy to get himself checked for prostate cancer or should I let nature take its course?

Dad shakes his hand, and takes a selfie with a big smile, "Big fan, Sir. Keep up the good work."

"Thank you."

Dad introduces us to the Premier. Mom shakes his hand next. It's a timid handshake.

It's my turn. I am frozen. I stay silent.

"What do you do young man?" The guy is charming.

"I'm a medical student currently doing a rotation in Calgary." My voice doesn't crackle. I feel confident.

"Really! What kind of doctor do you want to be?"

"Urologist. I have a special interest in prostate cancer. I plan to do research on the effects of prostate cancer in men in their 60s and 70s. Screening is available but underused."

"Maybe I should get checked."

"You should." I lied about the whole prostate thing. But if a lie saves his life, I think it's worth it. What do you think?

Premier shakes my hand and moves on.

Dad is standing in front of me and giving me angry looks.

"You want to be a urologist?"

"Maybe, maybe not."

"Did you lie to him?" Dad is not letting it go.

"It's not as if politicians don't lie to us."

Dad doesn't respond. Dad goes into the crowd to shake more hands. Mom and I are left looking at the spectacle of power and greed.

CHAPTER 20

The drive home is accomplished in silence. Dad is basking in pride. He got all the attention from those in power. His subtle smile says it all. He's driving vigorously. Power does that to people. Mom keeps her eyes closed. Some sort of meditation I suspect. I have become a walking and talking CT scanner. I'm missing a radiology reference. I spend my time looking for radiology apps, only the free ones. I find a couple, plenty for me. Technology is a wonderful thing.

Dad is confident in his driving. His driving record says otherwise. He's three demerit points away from suspension but never gets there somehow. He fights each driving ticket in court. Never wins. Technology also helps him. He has a night vision camera in his car, among a plethora of other safety features.

Dad had a glass of wine. I kept a close eye on him. He is safe to drive. That's my subjective opinion. If he gets stopped by a cop, then the alcohol meter will really tell the story. We reach home without an incident. I'm relieved.

I'm ready next morning at 8:00 AM sharp. Corn flakes is my breakfast. Simple yet fulfilling. Mom and dad are still asleep. I knock on the bedroom door. I say goodbye to them in their bed.

"Why so early?" Mom rubs her eyes.

"I have a lot of work to do today. I have to catch a flight at night among other things."

She doesn't argue. Dad doesn't even bother.

No shenanigans on the road. I keep it in the right lane, strictly under the speed limit. I pass three police cruisers with speed traps. Not this time fellas.

I park the car in the underground garage. It's eerily quiet in there. It's Sunday. People wake up late. I don't like lonely parking lots. Not in a big city. Anything can happen. Summer brings out people for good as well as bad things. It's not a statistical interpretation of crime statistics but a hunch, take it for what it's worth.

I can hear the echo made by my footsteps. It's that quiet. There is a black SUV parked at a distance. Windows Tinted. Maybe a Cadillac Escalade. It's too far to be sure. Doesn't matter. Two guys come out of the vehicle. Both are wearing hooded jackets. Young, race unknown. Skinless means raceless to me.

I pretend to ignore them. I turn around and make my way to the exit. I can hear their footsteps getting closer to me. There's only one exit door. We are all heading there. Nothing to worry about yet. Maybe they are in a hurry. But there is another possibility. What if they are the bad guys? My idea of dealing with danger is to run, not fight. My hands are soft like a baby. They are meant to cuddle and reassure, not throw a punch. But even a baby can bite. If it comes to a do-or-die situation, I'll do what I must do.

I have a plan. I'm going to turn and go back to my car and let the guys exit the garage. I take a left turn and walk in the side lane avoiding any eye contact with the guys and reach my car. No sign of them yet.

I am smart, aren't I? I get a jolt. The guys are standing in front of me, ten feet away. Both are staring at me. They mean business. I am the target. No doubt about that.

"So, you think you can get away just like that?" the tall guy says. He's at least two inches taller than me. Probably ninety kilograms. The abundance of fat, muscles, anger, courage, and criminal intent.

"Excuse me." I keep it soft.

The tall guy smiles. Yellow teeth, silver fillings. Worryingly he has a loaded gun in his back pocket.

"You can turn, you can walk, you can run, but you can't hide." He has a Canadian accent, whatever that means.

I was not running, certainly not hiding. I was avoiding whatever fate had in store for me. Of course, I don't say it out aloud. I value my life.

"You called the cops on our guy at the airport. We can't let it go. It's payback time." It's the shorter guy's turn. He is three inches shorter than me. I am a good reference point to measure heights. He has arthritic knees. I can outrun him. He has signs of previously healed fractures, probably involved in a lot of fights. A veteran criminal. He's not carrying a gun. Not even a knife. He has stashes of cash in the jacket. A senior gang member. He directs, doesn't shoot.

"I don't know what you're talking about." I plead ignorance.

"You think we're stupid. We have been tracking you since the airport. You thought the guy with the drugs was alone. You were wrong." The tall guy rubs his hands. He enjoys killing people.

"I think you got the wrong guy. I have snitched on nobody." I lie with the conviction of a politician. I got motivated by hearing Mr. Oilfield's speech. A lie repeated many times would replace the truth. I'm hoping for that.

"We are wasting time," the short guy chastises the other. "Let's finish the job before someone else walks in."

I'm desperate. It's the fight of my life. I don't have the physical strength to take on professional hitmen. I don't have experience. I certainly don't have the courage. I do have one thing, insight into them. My eyes are fixated on the gun. I can't let it be discharged. I must grab the gun. I need a distraction.

I shout, "Police!" I look at the back of the assassins. They turn their heads. Typical.

The bluff works. I lunge forwards and reach for the back pocket to grab the gun. The bluff is over. My hand is intercepted by the tall guy. Tall guys have long hands, you know.

The guy has a firm grip on my hand. I can't move it any longer. My wrist is being squeezed. The tug of war is not going anywhere. I am not letting it go and nor does he. I bear the pain of his strong grip. My hand is on the barrel but that's of not much use.

He makes his next move. He grabs my neck and puts it in a chokehold. He's tightening the noose. Before I collapse, I must let go of the gun and deal with the most serious problem at hand.

I see his internal carotid arteries, full of plaque. They are narrow. Nice. I grab his neck as well and both my hands land on the carotid arteries. The blood supply to his brain is cut. I squeeze them and see a plaque dislodge and go to the brain.

He closes his eyes, his grip loosens, and he falls to the ground. As he falls, he lands on his head and breaks his skull. A bonus. The gun remains hidden behind his back as he lies morbidly on the floor.

I barely catch my breath when I get punched in the gut. I bend and wince in pain. The short guy throws two tight slaps on my cheeks in quick succession. My ears start ringing. What kind of martial arts is this?

I throw punches too. He ducks, I miss. He grabs me by the neck with both hands. I kick him in the groin. He doesn't show any emotion, but his grip does loosen for a few seconds, and I take a deep breath to get reserve oxygen.

He regains his strength quickly and I'm back in the chokehold. I see no problem in his arteries. I put my hand on his neck, but my grip is too weak. He doesn't budge.

My eyes are desperate to find something wrong with this guy. His arthritic knees don't cut it. I see a sharp bony spur on his neck. It's close to the spinal cord. I punch at it. The spur cuts through the spinal cord like a steak knife.

He rolls his eyes and falls to the ground. The nerve connection from his brain to his body is cut. He too lands on his skull and gets a subdural hematoma. The bottom line is both guys are on the ground fighting for their lives. Death is at their doorsteps.

CHAPTER 21

I sit down on the ground and shout. It's a defense mechanism to relieve stress. I cry as well. I take a deep breath. I scan my body for any damage. I can't see the skin, but my neck and gut structures are intact. My muscles are beginning to swell. No biggie.

I look around. No one is in the garage. I am sitting on the ground, surrounded by two, almost dead people. I know it's not a laughing matter, but I won't judge you if you do. My first instinct is to check the guys for any pulse and maybe do CPR. That's what the Hippocratic oath does to you. I'm also reminded of the fact that I am not a doctor yet. I haven't taken the oath formally. To hell with them. I mean they're going to hell anyway. These guys are certainly eligible.

I have won the fight. Is it the first of many? I don't know. The bad guys know who I am, where I am. They can find me again. I have snitched on them. I have killed two of their members. Revenge is in order.

I don't want any police security. It only suits politicians and celebrities. I value privacy even though the big tech knows more about me than my parents.

I call 911.

"I need help."

"What happened?"

"Two guys attacked me."

"Are you in danger?"

"Not right now."

"Where are the guys?"

"Lying in front of me."

There was a pause.

"Excuse me."

"They attacked me, I responded in kind. Both guys are on the ground, unresponsive."

"Dead?"

"Don't know."

"Are you hurt?"

I pause.

"Yes, I am. The guys tried to choke me and punched me. My neck and gut hurt."

It's wise to exaggerate symptoms, it never hurts.

"Where are you right now?"

"West End Apartments, underground garage."

"Don't worry, dispatch is on the way."

The police and the paramedics arrive in under five minutes. I lie flat on the ground and groan in pain. It's acting 101. It helps to create empathy. First impressions matter.

"Are you OK?" A paramedic asks calmly. These guys have seen it all.

"My neck hurts, my gut hurts."

The paramedic stabilizes my neck with a collar, checks my vitals, and does a head-to-toe exam. He verbalizes findings to a colleague.

The other paramedics check the guys. They are presumed dead.

A cop closes in on me.

"What happened?"

"I was coming out of my car. These guys came out of the black SUV and attacked me. They grabbed me by the neck, punched me, and wanted to shoot me."

"How come they are on the ground lying dead?"

"I defended myself. I grabbed the tall guy by the neck as he was choking me. He collapsed suddenly. The other guy then tried to choke me as well and I hit his neck and he fell on the ground."

The cop has a perplexed look on his face.

"Are you trained in combat?"

"No, I'm not."

"So how do you explain all this?"

"I guess I was lucky if you call getting involved in all this luck."

The cop is unimpressed.

I groan with pain, holding my gut.

"Are you alright?" A glimmer of empathy from the cop may boost my defense. It's psychological warfare guys.

"Why would they attack you?" The cop wants to be a detective.

I want to say the word targeted but it's a loaded word.

"I called the cops on a guy carrying drugs at the airport. Maybe the attack was payback for that."

"Targeted. Where was that?"

"Calgary airport, on Friday. It was in the news."

A paramedic interrupts the cop. "We need to get going. He needs to go to the hospital."

"What about the other two?"

"Dead. Call the coroner."

I wish I could do an autopsy on these guys. I know what happened to them, but it would still be fun to open them up and grab their organs in my hands. Alas! it shall remain my wish only.

I'm attached to the monitor. My vitals are perfect, 120/80 bp, heart rate 84, breathing rate 18.

The ambulance is cutting through the traffic. Cars give the right of way to the ambulance as they should. I feel important.

CHAPTER 22

I'm at the Toronto Trauma Centre. I tell the same story to a nursing student, nurse, medical students, junior resident, senior resident, and finally to the attending physician. I don't get bored or irritated doing the same thing repeatedly, sort of like Broadway actors. They keep doing the same play for years. I now know how they must feel.

I want the CT scan of my head done. I know how to fake symptoms to get the alarm bells ringing. The worst headache of my life is good enough. I get rushed to do a CT scan of my head and neck.

I'm curious to know the results. I want to know if my brain has any organic changes from the curse that has made the skin disappear.

I got a room in the ER. Some semblance of privacy. When I say room, it's a cubicle with a curtain on the door.

I text my girlfriend. I call mom. They're on their way. I will minimize my symptoms. It's the right thing to do. Why create panic?

Sawaal is the first to arrive. She hugs me tightly. Her eyes are a bit damp. It's a sign of love and affection. Reassuring.

"How are you doing?" She asks me as she holds my hand. There is warmth in her hands.

"Alright."

Then she goes into lawyer mode. When, where, why, how? I tell her the truth, not the whole truth but just enough.

"You killed two people?" Her voice has concern for me.

"I did. They wanted to kill me first. Should I have let them kill me?" I'm getting annoyed.

"You have a strong case. I'll ask my mentor, Mr. Henderson. He's a top criminal lawyer in the city."

"Thank you. Do you think I'll be charged?"

"Unlikely, but it's better to prepare for the worst."

She taps on my shoulder," Don't worry, everything will be fine."

I'm glad she's standing with me through thick and thin. I am proud of my choice.

"My parents are coming anytime."

"I'll get going then."

"I didn't mean like that."

"You need alone time with your parents. I need to get going on the self-defence case."

"Thanks for being supportive and understanding."

She kisses me on the cheek and gives me a

reassuring smile on the way out.

My parents arrive thirty minutes after her departure. They make a dramatic entrance. Mom is a drama queen. She doesn't hold back. She did get a drama certificate in school which she proudly displays at home along with her medical degree. It's being put to good work today.

I hear someone taking deep breaths outside the room. It's Mom.

"Are you OK, my baby?" Mom asks, standing at the door as she rushes to hug me.

"I'm fine Mom. You see, no IV lines, no monitors. I can't be that sick."

I am in a hospital gown which gives me a sick feeling.

"This city is not worth living in." Dad stays stone-faced. "Crime is running rampant, yet the economy and civil liberties are crawling."

He's not a politician but behaves like one.

"Dad, it was not random. I was targeted."

"Why?" Mom's eyes are popping out.

"Are you involved with bad people?" Dad interrogates me like a detective.

"I called the cops on a drug dealer at the airport. I was being a Good Samaritan. That's all."

"Why didn't you mind your own business?" Dad chastises me.

"And we let criminals run the society?"

"You are no Gandhi."

"I'm not but I can't close my eyes to crime."

"Look where it has got you."

"I'm fine. The guys who attacked me lost much more."

"Did they get arrested?"

"They're dead."

"What?" Dad is showing some emotion. Mom is left speechless.

"You killed someone."

"Yes, I killed a criminal. In self-defence. Nothing is going to happen, Dad. I had no choice. It was my life against theirs."

"What did the police say?"

"Nothing yet. They will investigate. Sawaal is confident that I have a strong case. She will arrange a lawyer if it comes to that."

"How did you get the strength to hit someone, let alone kill someone?"

"You underestimate me, Mom."

"But you can't even kill a spider at home."

"I've grown up."

The family conversation is interrupted by the ER resident. He comes with a team. Attending Physician is missing. That's a teaching hospital for you.

"Mr. Sidhu, how are you feeling?"

"I am better."

"Good. Your results are back. CT head is normal, so is C spine X-ray."

"Thank God." Mom folds her hands in prayer.

"You're good to go." The ER resident signs off on the discharge papers. He gives it to his junior.

"Can I see the CT scan report?"

"Sure." The resident is taken aback. He's not sure if he should show me the result but he has no choice. I have the right.

It's a preliminary report. The impression is to the point. No acute abnormality. There is a comment on the oversaturation of images which reduces the sensitivity of the exam. The same thing happened during the retinal scan. Something spooky is going on inside me, it's organic, not some stupid ghost, that's what I believe anyway.

The ER team leaves. There are plenty more patients to see than waste time showing empathy to me.

"What now?" Dad asks.

"I still have a flight to catch Dad. It's in three hours. I can still make it."

"Are you crazy?" Mom says, ironic coming from a psychiatrist.

"There's nothing wrong with me. I must finish my rotation. I see no point in getting a sick leave."

"If you feel up to it then go ahead." Dad understands the ambitious drive. He hasn't missed a day to do scopes in the last five years.

"I think you should go now. Don't worry about me. I need to get going. I must go to my apartment and then I'll take the train to the airport."

"OK, OK but please call me on reaching

Calgary." Mom seeks reassurance from me.

"And mind your own business." Dad is blunt but right.

I nod.

CHAPTER 23

I get a taxi, can't risk public transport. I reach the apartment building. My eyes scan all around. I know I'm being watched. I take the empty elevator. The elevator reaches the tenth floor. I look around, no one is there, all clear. I run. I can't find the key, damn it. I have so many keys in the key chain, all look alike. Hurry up, man. I curse myself. I should have been prepared. Stupid. The first two keys don't fit, the third one opens the door and I slam it shut from the inside. I take a deep breath.

Paranoia. Yes, but justified. Don't you think? I collect my belongings, one carry-on bag, which doesn't take too long. I have the urge to carry a knife with me. Nah! Taking a knife to a gunfight is stupidity and taking a knife to an airport is heights of stupidity. I give up.

I take a taxi to the airport. The lineup for check-in is long as usual. I'm not going to snoop around other people's luggage. Mind your own business is thought of the day. Every day.

I look, I ignore, and I move on. It sums up

my check-in experience. I board the plane, window seat as usual. A middle-aged man occupies the aisle seat. He's wearing a suit. A white collared guy. A briefcase is tucked underneath his seat. I can't resist, I peek through, papers mostly, I can't read.

He's on the heavier side, typical North American. Mind your own business, man. I pick up the airline magazine, boring and germ-laden. I put it back. It's better to look outside the window, that's what a window seat is for, isn't it? There's not much of a view outside. Luggage is being loaded, it's boring and predictable but at least it occupies my mind.

The flight takes off and is above the clouds in no time. The meal service begins promptly. The crew wants to get it over with. It's short, nothing is free. Most pass. Not the businessman. He orders a burger and a cold drink. I ordered tea, with skim milk and a sugar substitute.

He's enjoying his burger. I'm not surprised. Chewing, not gulping. Licking his fingers, yuck! He's less than a hundred burgers away from getting angina. The fat-laden arteries are doing their best to pump the blood through the body. He looks at me and smiles. I reciprocate and look away. Mind your own business. He probably knows he is not going to live much longer if he keeps this lifestyle. His life, his decision.

I have enough problems of my own to give unsolicited dietary advice to this guy. I'm a marked man. The kind of attention I don't want. I must worry about every step I take. It's exhausting.

I spend the rest of the flight staring out of the window seat. The miracle of flying cannot be underestimated. Flying over clouds makes us all angels. The power that only God could possess in ancient times and here we are bored to death on a long-haul flight waiting for the sleep strike.

The flight lands on time. I'm eager to get out of the plane. I treat every stare with suspicion. I walk fast. I'm out of the airport in no time but there is time to get the flashbacks. It's where I signed my own death warrant. Whether I am shot by a sniper from a distance or point-blank to my head is getting lost in detail. The result is the same. I don't want to die. Not until I get married, have kids, watch them grow, see them get married, have grandchildren, enjoy retirement, and see my body decline before my eyes. I don't want to lower the average age of a typical Canadian male.

My first stop is not the temporary apartment. I stop at Best Buy and fill the cart with surveillance cameras. The next stop is the hunting store, buying bear spray won't hurt.

I set up the room and install the cameras. Getting ready for the intruder, Home Alone style. One thing I forgot, putting the warning label on the door, 24-hour video surveillance. I print the label and put it on the front door and on the windows of my seventh-floor apartment. It's paranoia all right but put yourself in my shoes, could you sleep at night if you know what I know?

I can't sleep. I lay awake, bear spray and kitchen knife by my bedside. The table lamp is on, to let them know that I am ready. Do not dare come.

It's wishful thinking. It's a bluff. It's a deterrent. I admit that assassins can always wear a mask. There are bank robberies every day in front of surveillance cameras. But maybe if I can make an assassin think twice before coming in, it's worth it.

I don't know when I slept but the alarm wakes me up. It's 7:00 AM already. Time to get ready. New day, new dead body, new autopsy perhaps, and new trouble, perhaps not.

I meet Dr. Gore in the cafeteria. He starts his day with a strong coffee, black coffee. I order a latte. He's without his entourage. I have some alone time with him. I can perhaps gauge if he would give me a stellar letter of recommendation. I haven't done any stellar work though. Regardless, this rotation has been life-changing, literally.

"How are you, young man?"

This is how people with authority speak.

"Alright, I guess."

"You must guess? How was the weekend? Did you go back to Toronto?"

"Yes, I did. Let's say my visit was eventful."

"Hmm."

I want to impress him, not scare him. I'll tell him a censored version of the events.

"I got assaulted in the parking lot at my apartment. Luckily, I got only bruises and aches and pains. Nothing serious."

"I'm sorry to hear that. Big city crime, random and senseless. Are you OK?"

His voice doesn't ooze empathy but it's better than nothing.

"Yes, I'm fine. I want to forget the incident. I want to move on. I don't want to take any time off. I want to finally do an autopsy."

"Good for you."

I hope I got some brownie points.

"Do we have an autopsy to do today?"

"Yes, we do."

It's music to my ears. It's a different matter that I can see inside the body without opening it. But the journey is more important than the destination.

"What's the case?"

"Not a mystery. A young man died in his apartment. Narcotics were found in the room. The family insists on an autopsy. We'll oblige."

"A drug overdose?"

"What else? But we will do the autopsy anyway."

We head to the autopsy room. I like the exclusivity. No distraction from other rival students.

The body is lying on the table. It's covered with a white sheet. Quiet and still. I would like to sleep like that. We all would one day but I want to wake up after such sleep.

I start my exam from head to toe, that's the

protocol. I can't examine the skin. I would miss any marks of struggle or tattoos. That's a bummer. But I can see what's inside.

I know how he died but I'll keep it to myself for now. I describe my findings to Dr. Gore. I give fabricated skin findings, maybe I'll be able to get away with it. He doesn't correct me. My guess was correct.

The procedure of opening the skull, chest, and abdomen is messy. I take out the organs one by one. It's a weird feeling to have someone's heart in your hand. It's slippery, I don't want to throw it on the floor. I squeeze it, there's no resistance. I'm not some pretty face or a scary monster to make the heart start beating again. Even if I was, there's not a chance it would. I should be careful with my words, look what happened to me last time I did an autopsy.

We take blood samples. I feel the paperwork. That's what medical students do.

"What do you think happened?" I ask.

"I told you what my hunch is, let's wait for the results. Do you have anything to add?"

I don't think he cares what I have to say but as a teacher, he must pretend to be interested. If I'm wrong, which he thinks I am most of the time, then it would give him immense pleasure to correct me.

"I think the guy had a pulmonary embolism."

"Oh!" Dr. Gore is taken aback. "Why?" There

is irritability in his voice.

I must tread carefully. To keep him happy is more important than being right.

"Let me show you."

I take the right lung from the jar and open the bronchial vessels with a scalpel.

"These are clots. Interesting. How did you know, you just opened the vessels right now?"

I can't tell him the truth. I tell him a reason that is plausible and half true. I'm not going to tell him which part is true.

"I searched for the patient profile in the system. He had been in the hospital last year. His hemoglobin was markedly elevated. He was a smoker, but polycythemia remains a possibility."

"Good work."

"I got lucky." I underplay my ability. It's a good strategy.

"Luck favors the smart."

I give a shy smile.

"I have a meeting to go to. You can write up the case and I'll sign it later."

"Sounds good."

Job done. My prospects for getting a stellar letter of recommendation have brightened.

CHAPTER 24

It's time to treat myself. I may not deserve it, but I need it. I'm hungry. I'll go to a restaurant for brunch. I want something homely. An Indian restaurant would do. Buffet would entice. A low bill would suffice.

I search for nearby restaurants. There are plenty but I go for the one with the most positive reviews. It is expensive but worth it. Not music to my ears but I am tempted.

It's within walking distance. I am there in ten minutes. The restaurant is posh and full. Popular, a good sign. I go inside. Two pretty girls in sarees throw flowers at me. They fold their hands to say namaste. Pampering. I'm a fellow desi. I don't need pampering, save it for the white guy.

I am given a table with a street view. I like the view of the bustling street and I can keep an eye out for any danger. There is pleasant classical Indian music in the background. Not too loud, just right. Portraits of ancient kings and queens on one wall and modern Bollywood celebrities on the other.

The cutlery is gold-plated. I am given a bowl of warm water with lemons to clean my hands. A warm towel to wipe them. The menu arrives. Alas! No buffet. Prices are exorbitant. Nothing is below twenty dollars, not even an appetizer except maybe for a cup of tea. Occasionally it's ok to splurge. I order butter chicken with plain naan, a safe choice. I don't want to order something new and exotic and regret paying for it later. A mango lassi for drink and mango ice cream for dessert. You may have guessed I like mangoes. Food tastes good. Not spicy, not bland, just yummy.

After a heavy meal like that, I need a siesta. Not much to do today at the hospital. A nap for a couple of hours would do wonders for my motivation. There is a card on the table to remind customers to review the restaurant. QR code is right there to make it easier for the customers. Good strategy. I ignore it. Enough with surveys, polls, and reviews.

I ask for the bill. Why do customers have to ask for it? It's eighty-nine dollars. I make it ninety-nine dollars with the tip and tax included. At least it's not a hundred dollars. It's psychology and I fall for it. I pay by credit card. Giving cash feels wrong.

I am not going to leave the restaurant without using the washroom. It's my right. The sign on the washroom door says, only for patrons. I am eligible, and I enter without any hesitation.

The washroom is clean, and not smelly. I

would post a good review. I am happy to see my skinless face in the mirror. A good day finally.

I come out of the restaurant. Sun is shining. The wind is calm. I am relaxed. I wait on the sidewalk. I'll take a taxi. Too full to walk.

I am pushed from the back. Before I look back, my arm is grabbed, and I am pulled into a van. It's all too quick for me to react. I am not a rabbit or a squirrel. I am the guy who couldn't walk home after a heavy meal. I get caught at my weakest point. Bad luck.

I am on the floor of the van. It's driving fast. I hope it speeds and gets caught by cops. It doesn't. Where are the cops when we need them? I am blinded by putting on a face mask, so they think. I can still see but I don't say. I can't say as my mouth is gagged in case I shout. Smart people or just standard procedure of kidnapping.

I am pulled up to a seat. They put a seat belt on me. Safety first. My hands and feet are tied with a synthetic rope. My mind is not. It's running faster than the old decrepit van. Its diesel fumes are suffocating. The kidnappers are masked as well. They are coughing from the fumes. I can't. I have to swallow that diesel smell. Yuck.

There are four kidnappers in the van beside the driver. Wearing facial masks is redundant for me but they don't know. They have guns of course. Kidnappers without guns would be career suicide.

I'm not sure I'm being kidnapped. Do they want money or worse, revenge? It's not a random act. I can put a wager on that. I don't have many advantages. I can't put up a fight. I'm all tied.

I look outside the window. I know where I'm going. It alarms the kidnappers. They adjust the mask over my eyes. Fools. I keep on doing it. They give up. They think I'm playing with them. Let them think. They are wrong. This is my advantage. I'll keep building upon what I have.

The van is heading out of downtown and eventually out of the town. We are on Highway One West towards Banff. Are they taking me on vacation? It's a joke and if I tell them, they will freak out. I tell them anyway.

"We have been driving for a while. Are you taking me to Banff?"

The look on their faces is priceless. Even under the masks and without the benefit of seeing their skin, I can tell that they are freaked out.

"If you need to know something, we will tell you." The guy with big biceps and the tiny brain says.

They don't talk. They are busy with their smartphones. Behaving like teenagers. Maybe they are teenagers. The way they text, which is faster than I can think, makes me suspect that. Lack of plaque in the arteries and bones without arthritis point to their young age as well.

One guy is a drinker. His liver is big and fatty. It only needs a punch for him to bleed to death. It can't be said of the tall guy. He's perfect physically. His muscles are strong. Maybe he's mentally weak. It's unlikely though. These guys kidnapped me in the middle of the day in a busy downtown street. They have nerves of steel. Risk takers. The other guy is just like me, physically at least. Guns and criminal intent give him the advantage. They will make a mistake. I know they will. I'll be waiting.

The van leaves the highway and takes the exit to Banff. Are they crazy? Taking me from a business centre to a tourist centre is stupid. It's an impractical location. The van turns right to the opposite side of the city of Banff. The road turns to a muddy, unkempt trail in the middle of a forest. Now, these guys are making sense. The scenery is beautiful but the same can't be said of my situation. God is on my side if it exists. I'm the good guy here. Good guys always win, right?

The van reaches a log cabin. It's huge. Maybe it's a hotel but I suspect it's not. The place is in the middle of nowhere. No neighbors. The only noise is from a nearby water stream. It's picturesque but also a perfect place to kill and bury someone in complete privacy.

I'm taken inside. It's a working home. The kitchen and living room are well stocked. We climb the stairs. There are three bedrooms upstairs. Well-kept and cozy. I'm taken to one room. No beds, just two chairs with a side table.

I sit on one chair. There's already another guy all tied up in the other chair. The room is otherwise empty. There is a small vial with clear fluid on the side table next to the guy.

The kidnappers stand in line and in full attention. They put away their smartphones. They remove their masks. They don't talk to each other. They stare silently at the door. They are waiting for someone to arrive. Their hearts are beating fast. I can see their bladders getting full, an anxiety response. Someone powerful and scary is coming, their boss.

CHAPTER 25

I can hear the tapping of the boots. A six feet tall guy enters. He is surrounded by more men, muscular, scary, and armed. The guy must be in his 30s. He's wearing a T-shirt and jeans. Designer sneakers. A gold Patek. The kidnappers lower their gaze to show respect. Not exactly a military salute but it shows who's the boss. He acknowledges with a smile. He is behaving like a dictator, why shouldn't he? He has the power over my life and the others in this room. I hope he keeps smiling. An angry boss is a nightmare for everyone.

He ignores me. I don't mind. He goes for the other guy. He signals to his bodyguards to remove the mask of the tied-up guy.

"Do you remember me?" The boss asks.

The guy is shaking. He's exhausted. He mumbles something. I can't hear. Neither does the boss.

"Someone give this guy a coffee?" It's not a request but an order.

"Do you want me to go to Starbucks?" The

guy with ripped jeans says. Since there are so many guys, I'm getting confused. I'll start naming them. I'll call this guy Bob. Don't ask me why.

Others stare at him with indignity. Newbie. Stupid.

"Make it here if you please."

"Yes Sir." Bob realizes his mistake. He runs out of the room.

The boss touches the tied-up guy's hair and tries to curl it. Weirdo. The guy looks down. I can see he's disgusted and terrified. If he pees in his pants, I won't be surprised.

The coffee arrives. It's offered to the man. He takes a sip and whines. Too hot.

"Too hot, eh!" The boss says with a narcissistic smile.

"Have you had your tetanus shot in the last 10 years?" The boss asks.

"Excuse me." The man is puzzled and so am I.

"You have a burn. I don't want you to get tetanus."

"I don't have any burns."

The boss pulls the man's trousers and pours the coffee into his groin. The man screams. I gasp.

"Now you got one. We have an antibiotic cream as well. It will treat any infection."

The boss is sadistic. Not a good omen.

The man keeps silent. If he's cursing inside, I won't be surprised.

"Do you remember me?"

"I don't."

"Why would you? When you needed my money then you called me every day. Once you got what you were looking for, you vanished without a trace."

"Are you an investor in my fund?" The guy is a hedge fund manager. I don't have a lot of sympathy for these guys but I'm human too. I can't see a man getting tortured.

"Yes, I was. I saw your ad on the television. You were promising a twenty percent guaranteed return on investment. International investing. Growth stocks. Blah blah blah."

"Can I correct? We didn't promise a guaranteed return. We only said that we had twenty percent return on average for the last three years and we advertised accordingly."

"But your returns were nowhere close to that. I lost money. Big money. Fifty percent loss. Two million dollars. It's not chump change even for me."

"I'm sorry. It was not intentional. Things happen. Past performance is no guarantee for future returns. You should have read the fine print."

"Oh, so it's my fault. And why do you keep the fine print so fine that nobody can read it or understand it."

I'm starting to feel as if the boss is the victim here. Weird, isn't it?

"It's marketing. I tried my best. Sometimes

markets don't cooperate. It's bad luck."

"Don't give me this nonsense. It's deception. It's a fraud. I know you got condos in Vancouver and Toronto. It's not possible with the salary of a manager. You were siphoning off money from the investors."

"If you have any grievances, please complain to the regulators."

"Toothless regulators. I am not waiting for them. Justice shall be done, and it shall be done by me."

"It's against the law, you can't do that."

"You bet I can. You don't know who you have messed with. It was my hard-earned money. From selling hard drugs."

The manager doesn't respond. He's in trouble and he knows it.

"Get my briefcase," the boss orders.

Bob is the official valet. He gets the briefcase from the cupboard. It's a vintage hard briefcase that opens with a key. It doesn't need to be opened for me to see what's inside. There are no guns or grenades. Syringes, needles, lots of them. Is this guy a dentist? We shall see.

CHAPTER 26

Bob puts a briefcase on the side table and opens it up. The manager sees it and is horrified to see the syringes. All those sharp things will find their way inside him. His body hair get raised. An alarm call. I can see that from a distance even if the skin is invisible. He's in the maximum state of alarm. His body can't do much else to get ready for what's in store for him.

"Get the half-inch needle."

Bob gives the needle to the boss.

"It's not for me. Pleasure is all yours."

Life is sucked out of Bob's face. He grabs the manager's hand, not to put a ring on it but to insert a needle underneath the nail.

Bob's hands are shaking. Stress tremor. Criminals do feel stress even though they lack empathy. Bob pokes the skin. The manager doesn't scream but blood comes out of the finger.

"Look what have you done." The boss is not impressed. "Are you trying to check his sugar? Stop the bleeding for God's sake."

Bob struggles to find the gauze in the briefcase. He uses a handkerchief to press the wound. The guys around him watch the horror show. A young recruit is getting the dressing down. They're glad that they're there and he's here.

"Come here." An ominous sign for Bob. "Give me the needle."

Bob obliges.

"And your hand."

Bob's eyes pop out.

"Please," the boss says in a loud and shrill voice. Bob has no choice.

The boss holds the needle like a pen. His hand still and his mind focused. He grabs the index finger and gently pokes it.

Bob screams. Tears come out of his eyes. His knees buckle. He folds his hands.

"I'm sorry. I won't make that mistake again."

"Good. Try again."

Bob gets up and picks up a manual in the briefcase and a sketch pen. He marks the points on the manager's fingers while referencing the anatomy from the torture manual.

Bob does the countdown. Hits the needle on the spot every time. His tremor disappears. He's laser-focused on the hand. It does wonders to his self-confidence.

I don't have to tell you that the manager is in pain. How much? The worst ever. 10/10. He would rather get his tooth pulled without anesthesia than endure this pain. He doesn't say it aloud, but I can make an educated guess.

He makes his body stiff as a board but to no avail. He's clenching his teeth and bites his tongue.

"What do you want from me?" His voice is muffled by blood in his mouth.

"Revenge." The boss says it clinically.

"Please take whatever I have. Take my money. Take everything."

"You have illiquid assets. Time is money. I'm not going to wait for you to sell the condo."

"It will be a quick sale. I know."

"I don't trust you but trust me, you're going to pay with your life. Death is inevitable. I can give you a choice though. You can have a painful life, or you can have a painless death. The vial on the side table has poison. At any time, if you feel like you can't take it, have a sip and all your troubles will be over in a painless fashion. I promise."

Bob loses the rope for the manager to access the vial.

"If you try to stop me with your left arm, we are going to poke needles simultaneously in all your limbs. Understood." Bob has found his authoritative voice.

I look at my fingers. They are awash with nerve endings. I know what's coming my way. My pain threshold is low. I dread getting my teeth cleaned. How am I going to deal with this? I feel like crying. I hold back. I don't want to project myself into this morbid scene.

Bob begins in earnest. He has started

enjoying it. He looks at the boss for validation and gets a thumbs up. His chest grows by an inch. He doubles down on poking. It's fast, synchronous, and precise.

I want to punch Bob's face. Maybe one day I will. I close my eyes and pray to God. Give this poor man some strength and me some luck.

Bob points to another guy. He's the one with slow-rise jeans which show off his designer underwear. I'll call this guy Alice. I know it's a girl's name but if you know any physics then you know that if there's Bob then there must be Alice.

"Hey pal, you want to give it a try. My hands are getting tired. Is it OK boss?" Bob saves himself. Trying to be smart in front of the boss is suicidal. He knows it.

Boss nods. Alice comes forward reluctantly. The poking game resumes. I'm getting numb to it. But that's not the case with the manager. His nerves are not getting tired of firing the pain receptors to his brain. He would have been better off if he had neuropathy but his nerves are healthy and that's his downfall.

The manager grabs the vial. A devilish smile appears on the boss's face. Alice also stops. The manager brings the vial close to his mouth. He stops. He's thinking, to drink or not to drink. It's a terrible dilemma to have. The rest of us are watching. Would he or would he not. It's a betting question. I bet he would. What do I know? It's my first time in this kind of predicament.

The manager stares at it for a full one minute. It felt longer. The boss rolls his eyes. The manager blinks. He lowers his hand. The boss winks at Alice, who knows what to do.

Alice starts poking even harder. The manager has put the vial back on the table. He endures the poking for five more minutes before he picks up the vial and gulps it.

Alice moves back. Nothing happens to the manager. Was the boss bluffing?

"How are you feeling dear?" The boss asks.

"I want to die."

"Have patience. That's what you tell your clients right?"

A minute goes by. How do I know? Well, I have a watch, you know. The manager is still standing. I mean he's sitting but you know what I mean. It's anticlimactic but I'm happy for him.

The chair begins to shake. There is a tapping noise from the chair as it is being violently shaken. The manager is having a full-blown generalized tonic-clonic seizure. His limbs are jerking back and forth. A white foamy liquid is coming out of his mouth. His back extends and he's lifted off the chair. The ropes can't hold him any longer. The back of the chair breaks and he falls to the ground. He's choking. I can see the fluid entering his trachea. The heart is beating fast but can't keep up. The blood to his brain has stopped. He's dead. This is no fluke.

The boss comes closer to the manager's face,

"I promised to give you a painless death. I lied. I trusted you and got burnt. You trusted me and got what you deserved."

The boss leaves the room with a macho walk. He glances at me before he exits. Alice and Bob mop up the place. The body is picked up and removed. I'm left alone in the room.

CHAPTER 27

I don't mind being left alone but not like this, tied to a chair. It's uncomfortable. I feel helpless. Freedom to scratch oneself at will is underrated. I get it now. You don't realize how much your skin craves any touch. It becomes painful and brings frustration in a matter of seconds.

I move my body to create some wiggle room. These guys know how to tie knots. May not be Gordian knots but close. I rub my body against the chair. Finally, some relief.

I hear whispers. Maybe they're planning a customized torture program for me. Maybe not. I hear the closing of doors, starting of the car engine and the noise of the tires. Then silence.

There must be a couple of people to guard me. But I don't hear anything at all. Am I all alone? It's a scary prospect or maybe not. It may allow me to escape.

Who's going to look after me? I need food. I need water. And last but not least I need to go to the washroom.

Time passes. No one comes. I shout hello. The cloth over my mouth is no barrier, it's getting loose. My voice may be muffled but I can manage a high pitch. I shout, is anybody there? No one responds. I feel abandoned. Like a bedridden patient with no caregiver. I don't have a button to press to call someone. I do have a cell phone. They forgot to take it. It's on mute but it's there. If only I could get my hands on it.

My wallet is also there. They didn't frisk me. Amateurs. That's Alice and Bob for you. I hope they come back. It's easy to deal with idiots. Boss is a different story. I want to be as far away from him as possible. He's a professional killer and he enjoys what he does. A true monster.

My phone is buzzing. Thank God it didn't ring when the kidnappers were there. I have some luck on my side notwithstanding the predicament I am in. Dad will be worried. Mom will be in a panic. The girlfriend will be in distress. Police will be in pursuit. But do they have any leads? Maybe my kidnapping was caught on surveillance cameras. There are traffic cameras everywhere. Maybe the police can trace the van to the lodge. Maybe they can connect the dots. There are a lot of maybes. It keeps the hope alive but barely.

There are plenty of unsolved cases. I am not a celebrity. I'm not a child. No amber alerts. Just a routine case. Another kidnapping. Another routine investigation. It's the summer holidays. Staffing is minimal. Motivation is questionable.

The prognosis is guarded. Doomsday is nearby. If you ever get kidnapped, please make sure it's not during the holidays. But it's not up to the kidnapped person, is it?

It's not all gloom and doom. On paper, my situation seems hopeless but in real life, miracles can happen. I mean how could you explain what's happening to my body? My x-ray vision. It throws strategic analysis out of the window.

Speaking of windows, there are no windows in the room. Who designed this room? How can the city approve it? Who am I kidding? These guys are criminals. They can do anything let alone cover a window with drywall. I can punch drywall. It's not that strong. Dad gets nervous whenever I try to put a nail in the drywall. We have very few pictures on the walls at home. This knowledge can come in handy now. But my hands are tied. But maybe my voice can help. But who will hear me out in the woods? It's like being in space. Scream all you want, no one hears, no one cares.

It's hot in the room. It's summer. No windows so no ventilation. It was thirty degrees centigrade earlier. Hottest day of the year. I'm sweating. There is a silver lining, however. My body fluids are coming out in the form of sweat. It means my bladder isn't getting full. It means there is no urge to pee. What a relief that is. My irregular bowel habits which tend to lean towards constipation are an asset as well.

I must contend with thirst. It's manageable

for now. I can always swallow my saliva. It's a disgusting thought but I'm getting a crash course in surviving. Genes should help. We are wired to survive. We have survived thus far because we are the fittest. It's an inspirational talk that I need. A positive attitude goes a long way. It will help me overcome the tsunami of pessimism that's coming my way.

The other problem with being alone in a room is boredom. I'm so used to being on the phone all the time that without it, life feels empty. It's even more annoying when I know that the phone is in my pocket, but I can't access it. It's like being stranded on an island. There is an ocean all around yet no water to drink.

I know what time it is. It keeps me oriented. I don't want to get delirious. I regret not getting a smartwatch. I decided why spend money on it when I have a smartphone. I was being cheap. I regret it big time. It could have saved my life. I could have made a call. I am so angry with myself. Never again. If I come out alive from this ordeal, I would be getting a smart watch. It's a promise to myself.

I have this urge to know what's happening in the world. I used to check my email, news feed, and messages every fifteen minutes. Not knowing what's happening in the outside world is killing me. It's ironic as I should be more worried about telling others about what's happening to me. Habits die hard. If I am on my deathbed or if I ever get shot, I would still like to check my smartphone one last time. I don't want to leave this world with an unread email.

I tap the chair. It makes a loud noise. I want to see if anyone comes. No one does. I try to push the chair; it moves by an inch. My target is the door. It's closed but I'm not sure if it's locked. Inch by inch, thrust by thrust I make progress. Like a tortoise, I don't want to give up. It gives me a sense of purpose. A good way to kill time and save me. I reach the door in 120 minutes. The door has a lever, not a knob. Good. I can press my head against it. Turning a knob would have been impossible. But that's only half the battle. I still must pull on the door. I have my mouth covered with a cloth but can still use my teeth to make a grip.

I try to grab the door. I miss. I try again and again. Fifty times in total. Fifty-first time I pull it hard. The door doesn't open. I try to push. Twenty tries later the result is still the same. I shout. It's muffled but at least I can vent. I spent two hours with no result. It's beyond disappointing. I console myself. People spend their entire lives getting a dream job or getting a dream home and still leave the world empty-handed. What's my two hours' worth?

I can't remain in this position. When the kidnappers come, the door will be blocked. It could alarm them. I want to project vulnerability and apathy. I want them to lower their guard. I make a round trip. It takes less time but more energy.

I prepare myself psychologically. Distraction is one technique. I'm on a nice beach lying in the sun, looking at the waves. That's a good way to handle torture. If my mind is not there, they can do whatever to my body. If this technique doesn't work, I will use the religious path. I come from a faith that's rich in history and courage. Martyrdoms are celebrated. The worst kind of torture was inflicted on my ancestors. They smiled but did not budge from their faith. I'm not that strong but if I share certain genes then maybe I can persevere. I haven't done anything wrong. I'm the good guy here. Morals are on my side. If I die, will I be a martyr? I think so. That doesn't sound too bad. If I can shake the fear of death, then there is no obstacle I can't overcome.

I've done the pep talk. Hopefully, it will keep me strong but that's not enough. It's a battle. I need a plan. I will fight. I have done it before. Two professional killers tried to kill me. One had a gun. Both ended up dead. I can do it again. Why not? I will scan their bodies for any defects. Any bony spur, any disc prolapse, any organ cyst. If I find any, I will punch. If they bleed, they will die. I need to be patient. My time will come.

I'm exhausted after making a round trip tied to the chair and after doing mental gymnastics. I feel sleepy. That's not a bad thing. I'm not on a king-size bed. There is no memory foam. There is no fluffy blanket. There's only my tired body and mind. I close my eyes. Sleep is right there.

CHAPTER 28

I open my eyes. I slept. Six hours. Not bad. That's more than what I usually sleep. I was tired. My energy level is up. It would get even better if I could get a cup of tea. I know it's too much to ask. It's 7:30 in the morning. No signs of kidnappers yet. Hope they show up today. I'm waiting.

My eyes lie in wait,
My mind filled with hate,
Come and do your worst,
I'm all in with the date.

Misery creates poetry. I'm the living proof. It's a nursery rhyme alright. I am no Frost but it's a start.

I hear something. It's the sound of a diesel pickup truck perhaps. The sound is getting louder. Doors open and close. People talking, not sure how many. They are downstairs.

They haven't forgotten me. I won't say I'm happy, but I am relieved. The worst thing in the world is if no one cares about you. Even haters and trolls care about you. The noises are coming from the kitchen. Maybe I'll get something to eat. I can't order breakfast. I must contend with what I'm offered.

The door opens. I close my eyes. I moan and groan. It's fake. It's an act. Let them believe I'm at the end of my wits. It's a message to them; be gentle.

"Hello, hello."

I slowly open my eyes. Put on a sad face. It's Alice and Bob. I want to smile but I don't.

"Look what we got for you." Bob has a breakfast sandwich in his hand. Nothing fancy. Jam and bread.

Alice has a cup of tea in his hand. He unties me. I rub my arms. What a relief.

"Thank you," I say. This thank you has a meaning as opposed to the thank you we throw at others casually.

"No problem."

My phone buzzes. Bad timing.

"Oops. We didn't take away his belongings," Bob realizes his mistake.

"Thank God. If the Boss knew about it, we would be dead."

"Don't worry, I won't tell anyone." I try to earn a favor from them.

Bob looks at me with pity. "You don't worry about us. You have enough things to worry about."

It's true but I don't like the condescending tone of Bob. He empties my pocket. I don't like that either.

"Enjoy the sandwich." Alice spits onto the bread. There goes my appetite.

They walk away.

I drink tea. It's cold. It's sugar-free. I need fluids. It will do.

I look at the sandwich. Spit has seeped in. He spits in the middle of the sandwich. I eat around it. Strawberry jam. Excessive sugar. Lots of calories. Whole wheat bread. It is good. I leave the round spit-laden part on the plate. I can't keep it on the plate for too long. What if they come back and make me eat it?

I hide the remaining sandwich under the leg of the side table. It fits in well. They won't notice.

They are back in ten minutes. I'm done with food.

"You finished it all." Alice smiles.

"How did the spit taste?" Bob says with a smirk on his face.

I'll tell you when the time comes. I don't say that aloud.

"I want to go to the washroom."

They look at each other. Bob moves his finger in a semi-circular fashion. It means no.

"Come on guys. I haven't gone to the washroom in a day. Do you want me to pee and poo in here? Do you want to smell all of that?"

"That's fair. We'll take you to the washroom." Bob realizes that it's going to get messy if I don't go to the washroom.

They accompany me to the washroom. It's

across the hall from the door. A three-piece washroom. It's clean.

They come inside the washroom

"Are you guys going to watch me do it?"

"Why not?" Alice says with a straight face.

"People pee together at the urinals all the time?"

I do my thing. They are at my back.

"I need to go for the number two."

They shrug their shoulders.

"Come on, you can't watch me do it. I warn you. Either you wear a mask or I'm not responsible if you suffocate in here."

It's a warning. They are criminals. Not perverts. They agree to my request and get out but with a warning of their own.

"Don't act smart."

"We will shoot and ask questions later. Do you understand?"

I nod. I take my time. They knock on the door twice.

My response, "just a minute."

I got to finish what I started. I come out of the washroom.

"Do you have toothpaste?"

"Get out of here," Bob nudges me back into the room.

It was too much to ask but it was worth trying. I got to keep pushing.

I sit on the chair. They tie again.

"What now?" I ask.

"Our job is simple. Make you feel the pain."

"What are you going to do?" It's a question that I'm desperate to seek an answer for.

"I will show you," Alice says and swings a punch at my face.

It hurt like hell. My ears are ringing. I've never been punched like that before. I'm not a boxer. My teeth are intact though. I move my jaw. I open and close my mouth. Nothing is dislocated.

Bob slaps me. It's no less painful. Tears come out of my eyes.

"It's not fair. It's two against one and I can't even defend myself. Act like men. Let me lose."

I get a punch and slap again.

"What are you afraid of? I'm not a professional fighter. You guys may be strong but you're cowards."

I have launched psychological warfare. My taunts have landed on target.

Alice loosens the rope. Yes!

"What are you doing?" Bob is annoyed.

"Don't worry. Let's show this rascal what we're made of."

"It's a bait."

"He's no match for us."

I am freed. I get up. I form a fist and move back and forth. It's a freestyle fight.

I'm desperate to find physical faults in Alice and Bob. There are none. A sebaceous cyst or a lipoma doesn't cut it. It will be my will against their intentions.

They try encircling me. I try to keep them at the front. Alice throws a punch. I duck. Bob's kick is blocked by my hand. I am working like a missile defense system. One or two missiles can be intercepted but not a barge of incoming projectiles.

The first blow lands on my chest. Ouch. They are not heavyweight boxing champs. I'm not going to be knocked by a single blow, but repeated blows will add up.

I catch Bob's kick. He slips and falls. Doesn't hit his head. I wish he had.

I get gut-punched by Alice. It's one on one now. At least for a few seconds. There are no rules in this fight. I can hit below the belt and I do. Kick in the balls. He bends to his knees.

Wow. Both are on the ground.

They are in agony. They are angry. Bob pulls out his gun. I should have gone for that. A strategic mistake.

"Enough." Bob gives me the ultimatum. "Stay still or else."

Alice moves forward. He starts hitting me indiscriminately. Punches, kicks, karate chops, you name it. No bite. At least I don't have to worry about STIs. Who knows what these guys are up to? They probably visit brothels more often than they visit their family doctor.

I lie in a fetal position. Trying to protect what a man cherishes the most, head and genitals.

Blackness descends on my eyes. I'll faint. It

will be for the better. An unconscious man can't feel pain. That's the hypothesis.

CHAPTER 29

I wake up. I'm back in the chair all tied up. It's midnight. I have mixed feelings. I got beaten up. I'm still in their captivity but I put up a good fight. I almost got them if it was not for the gun. I'm still alive. That's what matters.

I survey my body for new damage. My muscles are sore and swollen as expected. No broken bones. Organs are functioning. No internal bleeding. No concussion. I may be down but I'm certainly not out.

I lay awake or rather sit awake. Sleep is nowhere to be found. What if I die? What happens to me? Is there a soul? Is there an afterlife? Is there reckoning? My insignificant life would be over. Nothing new in the history of this earth. Would I like to be burned or buried? I don't have any choice. These guys would bury me. Easy. Less messy. Police will find my bones decades later. A mystery will be solved. My loved ones would probably be gone by then. My picture would decorate the database of missing persons.

As you can see pessimism is absorbing me along with contemplation. I can't solve the age-old question if God exists sitting tied up in a chair. Nor can I analyze why my karma has brought me here. If God exists, it helps those who help themselves. I need to fight my own fight. Those sons of a gun, if I can get to their guns, my problems would cease and theirs would begin.

They are here. Chitter chatter. I wonder what they talk about. Me. Hope not.

"Hello," Alice keeps it simple.

"Sore eh!" Bob rubs it on me.

I nod. I validate. Maybe they will show some mercy. Not that I have high hopes.

"Here's your warm breakfast." Bob has a soggy bread and a steamy hot coffee in his hand.

They untie me and leave me alone. They don't spit on my sandwich. Maybe they did, not in front of me. It's a peanut butter sandwich. Gooey. Not appetizing at all. I can't swallow it without closing my nose. Coffee is hot. I have to blow into it to cool it. It's black. No sugar. I like it. Wakes me right up. I have the urge to throw it on their faces. It's risky. I drink it fully.

"Fancy a trip to the loo?" Alice pokes his face into the room.

"Yes please."

They accompany me to the washroom but don't go inside. They are learning. I am too. I do my thing. No number two today. Irregular bowel habits are the least of my problems.

They walk me back to the room.

"Sit," Bob orders. His hand is on the gun in his pocket.

Alice goes out of the room. He's back in a minute with a black bag. He pulls out a baseball bat and a hockey stick.

"What do you like, baseball or hockey?" Alice asks.

"Neither. I like cricket."

"What's cricket?" Bob is ignorant. Doesn't surprise me one bit.

"It's a game that originated in England but now the whole of South Asia is crazy about it."

"I don't care." Bob has no willingness to learn anything new. That's why he's stuck as a lowly criminal. I don't tell him that. I don't care about his career prospects either.

"Are you going to beat me with a baseball bat and a hockey stick?" I come straight to the point.

"Yup." Both say in synchrony.

"That's not fair. Give me a bat. I'll show you how to swing it."

"Why? Did the United States give weapons to Iraq or Vietnam to make it a fair fight? It's asymmetrical warfare, get used to it." Alice says. I didn't expect that from Alice. The guy is well-read but still stupid.

Bob takes the hockey stick. Alice has the baseball bat. They surround me. I use my palm to fend off their attacks. It hurts. I can't sustain it. I have an idea. I take off my shoes and put them on my hands. Brilliant. The key to defeating a stronger opponent is to improvise. Vietnam did it. I will too.

They swing it hard, but my sports shoes have good shock absorbers. I throw in a kick occasionally. It doesn't land anywhere but keeps them on the edge.

I trip Alice with my foot. He falls to the ground. Lands on his face. His tooth is broken. He's bleeding.

I charge on Bob with hands covering my face. I push him to the wall. His hockey stick cracks as I hit it hard with the shoe. He throws away the stick and grabs me by the neck. I hit him in the balls. He should have known. It's my favorite shot. He moans. I put my hand in his pocket. Gun will be mine.

Bang. Bang. My head. I…………

CHAPTER 30

I feel dead. My mind is numb. I can't remember what happened to me. I try to piece together the events. I was in some sort of a fight. With whom? I can't remember. There was a guy, no two guys. What were their names? I wait, I agonize. Why am I tied to a chair? Where am I?

I give up. Memory will come. I can't rush. I know my name. I know I'm in Calgary. I know I am a medical student. But why the hell I'm in this room? Relax? If it's a concussion, rest is the key.

My mind may be sore, but my body feels fresh and strong. I haven't felt like that in a long time. I'm ready to run a marathon. My muscles are bulbous and stretchable. Oh yes! I remember I can see inside the human body. I called the cops on a guy at the airport. I killed two assassins. I got kidnapped. I had a fight. Alice and Bob. I got hit on the head. I feel my head, no fractures. I feel good.

Another fight is coming. It may be the last one. Let them come. They know I'm not a pushover. I'm angry. I want revenge. It motivates me. A motivated opponent is dangerous. I'll hit them with the full force of my fury. God help them.

I checked my watch. Oh, my word! I've been out for three days. Maybe I was in a coma. If that's the case, I am lucky to be alive. Luck favors the brave and I have been brave. I did not submit to them. There's an invisible force that's protecting me. If it's divine or not I don't know. I should believe in myself. I should start taking risks. Enough with the life of fear and anxiety.

Bad boys are back. Their whispers are audible inside the room. Their hysterical laughter. Let them laugh. They may not get another chance. I've been tortured. I've been humiliated. I won't forget. They will pay with interest.

"Knock, knock."

"Anyone there?"

I don't respond to their childish pranks.

"Look who's alive?"

"You won't die, do you?"

Who said what I don't know, and I don't care. For me, Alice and Bob are the same. They deserve the same punishment.

"I am strong or maybe you're not up to the mark?" I'm in the mood to annoy them.

"Listen buddy, we have been taking it easy. You are going to get the VIP treatment today." Bob points his finger at me.

Alice gets the briefcase from the cupboard. He gets the manual and puts markers on my fingertips. He gets the needle in his hand.

"Now the real fun begins," Alice pronounces.

My muscles are tense. I grab Alice's hand. He's not alarmed.

"You can hold my hand. I know it hurts like hell."

He pokes my finger. I feel the prick but no excruciating pain. Not something I can't handle.

They look at me with anticipation. I keep a poker face.

Alice looks puzzled. He consults the manual. He pokes and pokes. I ignore.

He's frustrated. He pushes the needle into my finger. The needle gets bent. No blood. No penetration.

It's my turn. I squeeze his hand.

"Ahh." The sound I want to hear. Alice is in pain. I squeeze the hand with full force. There is a cracking noise. The bones in his hands are being crushed.

Alice doesn't scream. Only groans. He gets up and tries to pull away. He can't. I twist his wrist and push it towards me. It severs his hand at the wrist. He falls to the ground with the arm amputated at the wrist. He's bleeding profusely. He is panting. He puts his other hand on the wound to stop the bleeding but to no avail. The radial and ulnar arteries are gushing blood with great speed. He's seconds away from hypovolemic shock.

"Tourniquet," I shout.

Alice is in no position to help himself. He is

almost dead. Bob instead of helping him, points a gun at me. Selfish.

I don't have much time. I throw Alice's severed hand at him. It distracts him. I pull on the ropes. They break like cotton threads. I charge at Bob. I grab his gun and point it away. He pulls the trigger. The shot hits the roof.

I punch his chest. It breaks the ribs and one of the ribs punctures the thoracic aorta. He falls to the ground.

Both are dead or one heartbeat away from death. I'm not going to do CPR on them. They deserve their violent deaths.

But I don't deserve a culpable homicide charge. It's self-defence but it's also the second time. Their violent deaths with the severed hand and the rib piercing the heart would make my case complicated. How am I going to explain what I did? Where did I get this superhuman strength?

I need to get rid of the evidence. It means getting rid of their bodies. I will bury them.

I go outside the room. Then from room to room. There are four bedrooms upstairs, each with an attached washroom. All hardwood. Nice house. Expensive. Boss has some taste. He could have brought me to a dungeon but instead, I'm in a villa.

I go downstairs. There is a gourmet kitchen with a pantry. A large living room with coffered ceilings. Ten-foot ceilings. A powder room with an LED backlit mirror. California shades. The dining room with oakwood furniture. The basement is unfinished. Trust me I'm no real estate agent but when I see a nice house, I get distracted. I think I have ADD. I forgot what trouble I'm in.

There's no one in the house. I must find my phone and valet. I go upstairs. I check their pockets. No sign of my phone. I checked the cupboards. Nothing there either. I go downstairs. These up and down trips are going to make me tired. They must be in a safe place somewhere or could be in plain sight.

I check the living room and the breakfast table, but nothing. I check the kitchen. Finally, luck strikes me. They are next to the coffee machine. Lazy bums.

The phone is dead. I don't have a charger. Tough luck. There is no landline, and I can't use the cell phones of the guys I just killed.

I go to the backyard. There is a shed. It's a large wooden shed. Unlocked. I go inside. All kinds of goodies. I get a shovel. There is a dense forest beside the house. I find a spot about a hundred yards into the woods.

I go back to the kitchen. There are garbage bags on one of the shelves. They are extra-large and strong. That will do.

I put the bodies in the bags and tie them. I pull the bags down the stairs. They are heavy. They should be with each one being seventy-five kilos minimum. That's more than my weight. My back is not in the best of the shape at the best of the times. I roll the bags. Friction is less and so is the effort. I'm putting physics to good use. The guys are already dead, and dead people don't feel pain. I'm not being cruel to them. I confess I did kill them but that was self-defence. I'm not a sadistic person. Extraordinary circumstances have made me do extraordinary things.

I mop the floor upstairs. I get rid of the blood and any signs of struggle. I can't do anything about the bullet in the roof. It's a tiny hole, which may get missed. The gun is going in the garbage. So is the briefcase.

I search the house for any money and jewellery. I am not a robber, but I need money. They are not going to go to the police. They are criminals for God's sake. They are after me. They are angry at me. I can't make them more furious. All I find is a twenty-dollar bill. Shameful, not for me but for the boss.

I bring the bodies to the woods. I do it in stages, ten feet at a time. It takes a couple of hours. Next, I dig up the grave. It's manual labor. It's exhausting. It's not the physical burden but the mortal burden that's bothering me. I feel like a serial killer. I'm going from a good guy to a not-so-good guy. A grey area.

It's a huge risk for me. It may be deemed criminal. Even if their bodies are found sometime later, my self-defence argument could still stand.

The bodies are buried. I say a small prayer, first for myself, and then for the departed souls. I hope they don't turn into ghosts and haunt me. I don't believe in ghosts, but my recent experience has shaken my rigid scientific beliefs.

I have keys to the vehicle outside. The keys were also found near the coffee table. It's noon already. I'm hungry but I don't want to spend any more time in the villa. I find a granola bar in the pantry. I chew on it fast. It will give me some instant energy as advertised.

I go to the front yard. There's a pickup truck. I have never driven one. It shouldn't be difficult unless it's a manual. Thankfully it's not. I start the truck and I'm on my way. There is a GPS in the truck. I don't know where I'm going yet but all I know is I need to get the hell out of this place.

CHAPTER 31

I know where I'm going. The intersection says exit to Highway One or go straight ahead to the city of Banff. I'll go to Banff. I'll report to the police there. Rest is their job. I don't know where the police station is, but it can't be hard to find. I don't have my phone, but I have my voice. I can ask. We have become too dependent on technology that we have lost the human touch.

I enter the town. It's busy. It's summer. Plenty of tourists. Nice weather. What else to expect?

It's not easy to ask for a police station. It can alarm people. They may think I'm in trouble, which is true, but I don't want to tell them. Privacy, please. So, I'll make an excuse. A fender bender is a good one. A minor traffic accident is a legitimate excuse.

The first order of business is to find parking. There are parking lots alright, but they are full. I prefer street parking. I look for it. It's not happening. Five minutes in and I'm already frustrated. Why am I bothered about parking? It's not my pickup truck. I can enter any parking lot and park wherever I want. If the pickup truck gets towed, so be it. Not my problem. I enter a parking lot. It's unmanned, even better. I take the ticket. There is one empty parking spot. I park it. Not a perfect job but the other guy can at least open his door. Job done.

I walk towards the city centre. I enter a souvenir shop. It's full of useless stuff that appeals to tourists who bask in the momentary nostalgia of the city. There are a couple of tourists in the shop, they must be as they are looking at the useless stuff with amusement. I will pick a token gift. Then I'll ask for help. It will improve my chances of getting a useful tip. I don't want a freebie.

But there is a catch. What if the guy doesn't know? Then my money will be wasted but I can always return the souvenir. I look for the cheapest gift, a keyring would do. It's still worth a toonie. What the heck. I'll buy it. It's still a souvenir and a memorable one. This is a moment to remember in my life.

There's a middle-aged lady at the counter. Blonde hair. Some wrinkles but well hid under the makeup. A loose-fitting light green dress. Her eyes are on the door, not sure if it's in anticipation of a new customer or to catch a shoplifter. Either way, she's not busy on her cell phone. Old-fashioned. She should know about the police station.

I go to the counter and say hi with a straight face. She responds with a feeble smile. She looks at the keychain. She has an expression on her face that says I belong in a thrift store. I don't care. I need information. That's what I care about.

"How are you going to pay?"

"Credit card."

She's not happy I can tell. On a toonie, she must pay tax and a fee to the credit card company. May as well give it to me for free.

I feel bad. I should have picked something more substantial. It's not too late. And I see chocolates on the counter. I pick dark chocolate. A local brand. 7.99 dollars, expensive for what it is but I am hungry and in a charitable mood.

The woman is unimpressed. I tap the card.

"Receipt?"

"No thanks. Can I ask a question?"

"Yes," she says reluctantly.

"I had a minor traffic accident on entering Banff. I want to report it to the police. Do you know where the police station is?"

"Of course. Go to the end of the street and turn left. It's about 150 yards from there."

"Thanks a lot."

"But don't expect too much."

"What do you mean?"

"There have been cutbacks. Lots of complaints about the delayed police response."

"That's no good."

"Good luck. You need that."

What she said is true. She was helpful. I go to the end of the street. The police station is visible from the intersection. It's a small building. No more than a drug store. Not unexpected. You don't need a battalion to protect Banff.

I enter the building. There's no one in the waiting room. Only chairs, ten of them. I notice mundane details like these. They are wooden and sturdy. The room looks like a log cabin from the inside. Goes with the vibe of the town.

"May I help you?" The receptionist says.

All I hear is why the hell are you here? She's young. Probably in her 20s. Caucasian but with black hair. Coloured of course. She has red designer glasses which don't suit her bland black dress. Not overly friendly but pleasant.

"I'm here to see a police officer."

"I bet you are but why?"

"It's confidential. I only want to disclose it in front of an officer."

It may raise the level of urgency, but it doesn't.

She shrugs her shoulders. "You may have to wait a while."

"What do you mean?"

"It's summer. Calgary Stampede is this weekend. A lot of our officers have gone on duty there. I have one officer on patrol duty today. He's going to be back in, let's say two hours. Come back then or you can wait here. I'll page him."

"I'll come back in two hours."

I can't believe it. There's a wait for everything in Canada, from immigration to seeing a doctor. Emergency rooms and airports are the places where time crawls under the weight of bureaucracy, in keeping with Einstein's General Theory of Relativity. I had to even wait for the kidnappers to come and interrogate me and now the police, are also missing in action. Oh well, it's time for a stroll.

CHAPTER 32

I walk the streets of downtown. Small but charming. Dare I say a tourist trap, well it works. It's full of tourists. Souvenir shops, food joints, ice cream shops, and of course bars. What else do tourists need? I walk among the crowds and disappear. It's a good thing. I'm not sure if someone is following me. Unlikely but it's possible.

I walk up and down Banff Ave. I get bored after twenty minutes. I have time to kill. I walk along the Bow River and cross it over the pedestrian bridge. On the other side, there is a walking trail. The beginning of wilderness that most tourists crave for. I am no different.

The river is wide and likely deep. Water is clear and likely drinkable but I'm not going to drink it. The river is getting more agitated as I walk along with it. The voice from the rapids is getting louder. It has a calming effect. There are wooden benches along the riverbank. Thoughtful. Not many people along the trail. I continue walking.

There's no one around. It doesn't alarm me. Nature and me, that's what I want. I sit on a wooden bench. It's time to relax.

I sit and contemplate. There are many things to ponder over. Least of which is why I'm still alive? Where did I get the strength to sever someone's hand and rip someone's ribs? I have never learned martial arts. I don't even remember the last time I was in a gym. All I do in the name of exercise is to walk the corridors of hospitals and believe me it involves a lot of walking. Airports and hospitals have never-ending hallways. My hands get tired after half an hour of typing on a computer. How did I get this strength? It doesn't make any sense.

The wooden bench is rock solid. I grab the edge and try to break the wood. Ouch! It hurts so much. Where is the strength that I possess? I start thumping on the bench. Harder and harder. The pain becomes lesser and lesser. The strength becomes stronger and stronger. I have the urge to hit it even harder. And I do. I hit the bench with full force, and it cracks. What the hell?

There must be some explanation. Not that I found a credible explanation for my penetrative vision. It's time to put my vision to good use. I closely examine the tendons and nerves of my right hand. They are noticeably different from the left hand. They are bulky and more vascular. The only conclusion I can draw is more pain, more gain.

Pain is a stimulant that produces strength. Muscles, nerves, and skin adapt to that stimulus. I have no idea how it happens but I'm not complaining. It has kept me alive. A survival instinct. An evolutionary adaptation perhaps.

I must adapt my tactics. If someone wants to hit me, I should let that happen. They are inadvertently providing me strength. Only then my punches will land with devastating impact. Defense is the best offense. Counterintuitive I know but that's what I have got.

I'm hungry. Sitting idle on a bench without a smartphone does that to you. There's nothing else to do. For how long can I stare at the raging river and the tall trees and the Rocky Mountains? I can't hold my attention for too long. It's time to taste the local dark chocolate. $7.99 will be put to good use.

The front cover has a pic of Bow Falls on the front. It's not too far from where I am. 200 yards maybe. How do I know? The wooden sign says that. Smart. Tax dollars put to good use. Otherwise, without Google Maps I would have been lost. There's a tear here sign on the chocolate. Excellent. I hate when it's a pain to remove the covering. It takes the fun out of eating.

I take a bite. Bittersweet taste. I eat three squares and put the rest on the bench. Let it sink in, the chocolate that is. I'll take my time to enjoy the chocolate. It's like wine, small bites that excite.

I look across the river. I can see a moose. Haven't seen wildlife in a while. There were moose and deer crossings on the highway, but I've never seen actual wildlife crossing the road. That's my good luck. Moose is drinking water and doing a tapping dance. I wish I had my smartphone. It's worth posting on social media. I hear a rustling noise. Where is my chocolate? I look at my back.

"You got to be kidding me?"

A bear has my chocolate. It's a big grizzly bear. It's a Mama bear. There's a baby on its side. All points to danger.

I stand still. Like a statue. The only thing moving on my body are the hair which are raised. My heart is in top gear. It's pumping fear into my body. They've got what they came for. Why don't they get going? Mama bear wants to go but the baby has other ideas.

The baby bear approaches me. I am missing bear spray and a whistle. Should I shout? I hesitate. No one will come for help. But that doesn't matter. Shouting is to scare the bear. It's too late. The baby bear is sniffing me, my pockets. It's going for my crotch.

I snap backward. It's a typical guy response. Mama bear comes for me. Oh dear. I make a fist and start hitting the ground. I don't have much time, but I get five quick thumps in quick succession. Plenty for me. I don't intend to kill but only scare. I'm refueled and ready.

I don't run. I like face-to-face encounters. The reason may be that I don't have the confidence to outrun a bear. And while running I can't see what's on my back. Losing control scares me. I can still see inside the bear's body. It's not that clear but I can make out the organs. But I'm not going to put it to use. All I want is for them to go away and leave me alone. Not too much to ask.

As she comes into my personal space, I strike first. I push the Mama bear and shout. It gets startled. It turns away and the baby bear follows it. Thank God. No one got hurt and everyone got what they came for. A happy ending.

CHAPTER 33

I don't turn back. I'm going to finish the walking loop before heading to the police station. I head towards the Bow Falls. I reach there in ten minutes. It's nice. The water is clean, and the waves are exhilarating. Not Niagara Falls but still pretty, and not intimidating. I turn right towards the Fairmont Banff Springs Hotel. A beautiful and imposing building. I don't have the money to go for lunch there today. Maybe some other time. I don't encounter any more wildlife. I do see a couple. I warn them of the bear sightings. Call the police, they say. Not much use I want to reply but I just nod. There are posters giving information on how to report wildlife sightings. I try to pass on the responsibility to others, but they throw it right at me. My phone is not charged, I plead. Folks are suspicious. What the heck? I warned people. If they don't care, they'll know in the nick of time that I was right.

     I see a bus. Free shuttle to downtown it says on the front. I get excited to see anything for free. I get on the bus. My legs thank me. I thank the driver. I get dropped off at the intersection of Main Street and Banff Ave. The police station is visible from there. I am well past the waiting time of two hours. The officer must have returned by now. I hope he stayed there and didn't go away for another patrol.

I enter the station. Same lady, same attitude.

"How may I help you?"

She doesn't remember me.

"I was here earlier, and I asked to speak to an officer."

"Oh yes. We do have an officer on duty in the building. Take the stairs. He's in room 204. I'll buzz him that you are coming."

"Thanks."

I take the stairs. Portraits of past police chiefs, all of them with a stern look. All white of course. Not a happy place I imagine.

I knock on the door.

"Come in."

I open the door slowly. I'm not expecting to confront anyone but it's an instinct.

"Hi, I am Karan."

"Hi, I am Officer Blunt. Take a seat."

The officer is old. All grey hair. Plenty of belly fat. Not a surprise. The guy is munching on chips in his office. At least he's experienced. But is it a good kind of experience? I'll keep my fingers crossed.

"How can I help you?" He says looking up

through his reading glasses. I couldn't help but notice that he was doing a crosswords puzzle. What a job.

"I am Karan Inder Singh Sidhu."

"Yeah, I got your name. First name is fine with me. So, what brings you to my neck of the woods."

"I was kidnapped some days ago."

He's not startled but he is suspicious.

"How many days ago? Two days ago, 200 days ago?"

The guy has clearly left empathy at home.

"Not sure. I am still disoriented. Maybe a week ago."

"OK but from where?"

"Calgary downtown."

I was expecting that he must have known about my case. My picture would have been on TV. I would have been famous. Police across the country would have been looking for me. So much for my fantasy.

"So, what are you doing here?"

"I don't know. Please check the database and you will know my name."

"I know what to do. You get your story straight first."

The guy is annoyed. I don't think he has seen many kidnapping victims. So much for his experience.

"I have run away from the kidnappers, or they have released me. Either way, I'm out of their custody. And I'm still in shock. I can't think straight through."

I skip the bear encounter. It would have been counterproductive. He would have dismissed me as a prankster. I want to keep my story plausible.

"OK. Do you want something to drink? Coke, Pepsi?"

That's the level of empathy he's capable of showing but at least he's trying.

"No thanks."

"So, what were you saying?"

"Well, as I was saying I got kidnapped from Calgary downtown coming out of a restaurant. I was put in a van and blindfolded and tied. I was kept at various places. I was always blindfolded so can't give you the exact description of my hideouts. One day I was taken from the hideout and driven outside the city and abandoned on the outskirts of Banff. I realized that when the kidnappers didn't come to get me. My restraints were loosened, so I released myself and realized where I was. I saw the Banff sign and drove here. And here I am."

If it was the vaguest explanation, you have ever heard, I accept your compliments. That was the intention. I can't tell him the whole truth. I have no intention to be charged with second-degree murder. The corpses I have buried back in the woods should remain where they are.

"Hmm." The officer stares at me while munching on his chips.

"Want some."

"No thanks."

He's psychoanalyzing me. Doing his own lie detector test. He's going to fail. I know it.

"Your story is hard to believe."

"Why?"

"How come kidnappers suddenly released you? Did you pay any ransom? And why would anyone kidnap you?"

"I don't know why I was released. But I do know why I was kidnapped."

"Go on."

"I called the cops on a drug dealer at the airport. I saw drugs on that guy and reported it. The gang had to take revenge and so they did."

"I see. So why did they release you?"

"I don't know. I'm not Sherlock Holmes."

"I'm not Inspector Lestrade either."

The guy knows his literature. I'm impressed.

CHAPTER 34

He checks the computer. Presses a couple of keys. The screen remains blank. He keeps pressing random keys. Nothing is happening. He looks at the computer screen as if he's staring into the abyss. It's an old windows computer.

"Can I help?" I ask. The guy is clearly technologically challenged.

"Do you know how to start this damn thing?"

"Unplug it and restart." An obvious but genius answer from me.

"I know that much. Do you know how long it takes to restart this old baby?"

He pauses. I thought it was a rhetorical question but he's expecting a concrete answer.

"I don't know, maybe two minutes?"

"No Sir. Ten minutes is the minimum. Isn't it shameful?"

"Not sure I get that."

"I'll tell you why. Criminals have the latest smartphones and laptops, and the police are stuck with these decades' old relics."

"Cutbacks?"

"No, it's because of a stupid chief?"

He makes it quite clear how much he respects his own police chief. I don't want to get involved in petty police politics, but I have no choice. I got to listen to a disgruntled employee.

"What's wrong with the guy?" I realize it is a mistake to say it to him as soon as I say it.

"Where should I start? He was a junior to me. He trained and served under me and now he is my boss. How cruel is that?"

"It must be hard for you."

I show some empathy. Maybe he'll learn that from me. But I doubt that he can learn anything at his age. He's stuck in his ways.

"I'm close to retirement. I'm counting my days. Seventy-seven days remaining. I served for thirty-plus years. I got passed over for a promotion. And what did I do? Ask me?"

Another rhetorical question he's expecting an answer to. His loud voice makes it clear that I better answer it.

"What happened?" I ask with fake sincerity.

"I got speeding tickets. I have a history of driving license suspension. The police board deemed it a blemish on my character. What a load of crap. How does it affect my ability to lead the force?"

"I can understand." I've got a disgruntled cop. My bad luck is not giving me any break.

"And do you know what the current police chief has going for him?"

He is on fire. Rhetorical questions are coming one after the other.

"What?"

"The right skin color. You see he's not white." He uses air quotes to emphasize non-white.

"Excuse me." I'm non-white. I should be offended. But I'm beyond that, I want to move on but clearly, this guy is stuck on racial politics.

"What's wrong with being non-white?" I ask my own rhetorical question.

"I'll tell you what's wrong. We spend too much time and money on sensitivity training. I can't stand it. Affirmative action is caustic."

The guy has clearly no filter. That's his problem right there.

"I wish we had a colorless society." That I say with sincerity. As far as I'm concerned, it has come to fruition. I can't see any skin. How cool is that? But even if the society becomes colorless, there are still plenty of grounds for discrimination. Humans have an insatiable appetite for discrimination.

He doesn't respond to my remark. Thank God. We both stare at the screen. It's doing the start-up sequence. A bunch of mumbo jumbo of the software updates are happening. Finally, it makes a sound, and all is well.

He puts in the password. Try again message, appears. He tries again and again.

"Damn it, I always forget the password."

He calls the reception.

"Lucy, what's the password for the computer in my room?"

"YOUAREALWAYSRIGHT4EVER." She explains the capital and number sequence in the password.

I hear that. Finally, the database is running.

"I can't find your name."

I know there must be a spelling error. I hand over my driving license.

"Try my full name."

"Yes, there is a match."

He takes time to read my report. I can't see the report from a distance.

"Oh."

"What's wrong?"

"Nothing. Yours is a high-priority case. There's a high-profile detective assigned to your case. Detective Sheer. He's a rising star. Blue-eyed man of the provincial police chief."

"Is that a good thing?"

I don't know. I have never been good at politics. That's why I'm sitting here."

"What's next?"

"Let me call detective Sheer. You stay put."

He makes the call. All I hear is Yes Sir, Yes Sir. So much for his macho attitude.

"What did the detective say?"

"Good news. He's coming right away. He'll be here in two hours. He specifically mentioned that you do not call anyone, not even your family."

"Why not?"

"I don't know. I'm just a cop. I follow orders without question."

There is no point arguing with him. I'll speak to the detective directly.

"So, what do I do now?"

"You wait. You can sit in the lunchroom next door. It has a television. There's a computer with the internet. And there are snacks and drinks. All for free. Enjoy."

"Thanks for your help."

"Anytime."

He gets busy with his crossword puzzle. It is not what I expect from a cop. Surprise has become a norm in my life.

CHAPTER 35

There begins another wait. It's comfortable in the police lounge. There is high-definition big screen TV, free food and drinks, a comfy sofa, and a lack of uncomfortable stares. I catch on to the latest happenings in the world. Nothing much has changed, the same old partisan politics, celebrity gossip, and people complaining about other people.

I have my own list of complaints but I'm not complaining that I'm still alive. There is much to be thankful for. Trying to look at the bright side of life. Trying, that's all I can do.

I'm curious to know what happened in my absence. What kind of media exposure did my kidnapping achieve? Did people care that I was kidnapped? I google myself. Lots of hits. Most of the news is from the day of the kidnapping. There was surveillance footage that captured the van. There was speculation about the motive. A targeted kidnapping. No explanation in the news as to why it was considered targeted. That's unfair. It implies I'm somehow involved with the gangs. The police should have clarified it. They didn't. It sucked empathy out of my case. The police said they were on the case and appealed for more information. No leads so far, they said. My kidnapping didn't make a splash. How disappointing.

I know why my case didn't get the attention it deserved. There was a royal visit. The Queen visited Canada. The media was preoccupied with every move of hers. A commoner like me had no chance to steal the limelight from the Royals. And there was a royal scandal, who said what to whom, who's cheating on whom. That was enough to suck all the media attention. I became a victim of apathy. Bad timing for me. The media was busy chasing the Royals. Police were busy protecting the Royals. And the kidnappers were let off with ease.

My emotions are not black and white. Do I really want my case to be pursued hard? I'm in two minds about it. Of course, I want the perpetrators of the crime to be behind bars. I want the crime boss to be locked up for life. But a thorough investigation would open Pandora's box. I would have to explain the whole sequence of events. Bodies may get discovered. Bodies that I have buried. I haven't been entirely truthful to the police. It's not going to bode well for me. I want a mediocre investigation that is not too difficult to get in Canada. We thrive on mediocrity.

I hear a knock on the door. I wish it's the

detective. He's forty minutes early. An empty mind weaves all kinds of conspiracy theories. I want my mind occupied. Interaction with the detective may keep me busy and help me subdue the negative thoughts.

"Hi, is this Karan?"

"Yes, I am."

"Hi, this is Detective Sheer."

I'm relieved. The wait was killing me. The guy is handsome. As tall as me, maybe seventy kilos, flat belly, and blown biceps. He's wearing a light pink shirt with black trousers. The dark brown shoes are shiny. An Omega Seamaster on the wrist. He looks more like a hedge fund manager than a cop. He smells nice too. Expensive perfume. He's probably in his 40s. Few grey hair, here and there. Clean-shaven and military-style haircut. Looks dapper. Quite a contrast from Officer Blunt.

"I was hoping you will be there on time, and you are."

"I try to be on time. I value other people's time and I expect the same from others. Let me first ask, how you are doing?"

"I'm doing OK considering everything."

"Good. I am so glad to see you alive and well. You are brave and lucky to have come out unscathed from this ordeal."

"Thank you for your concern."

"It's my duty. You have been on my mind twenty-four hours for the past week."

"Good to know that you are that concerned. So do you want me to narrate what happened?"

"You must be tired. You don't have to repeat everything. I got notes from Officer Blunt. He's a jolly guy, isn't he?"

"Yeah."

"I have done background work and I have a good idea as to what's happening here."

"Do you? Please enlighten me."

I'm dying to know who wants me dead. I have some ideas too as to my enemies but it's good to get a third-party perspective.

"The guy who was caught at the airport was the brother of the drug lord Rob Bank. We believe he is responsible for your kidnapping. You were attacked by his men in Toronto. These guys are relentless. They don't give up that easily."

"Is the guy in prison?"

"If you're referring to Rob Bank, no he's not. His brother Terry is in jail pending trial."

"Tell me more about this Rob Bank."

"He owns the drug trade in Western Canada. His base is Calgary. He was born and bred in Calgary. He had a tough upbringing. His parents struggled to make ends meet. He was a bright kid and excelled in his studies. Even to medical school in Calgary."

"Really. He's a doctor?"

"Yes, it's hundred percent true. He went to UBC for anesthesia residency."

"What happened then?"

"I'm not a criminal psychologist. I don't know about his motivations, but I know the facts. He siphoned off drugs, wrote fake prescriptions, and overdosed a patient."

"Oh, dear."

"Obviously it ended his career. He got convicted and spent eighteen months in jail. And when he came out, he was a bona fide criminal. He joined a small gang of drug peddlers. He merged many gangs to become their leader."

"He acquired assets to become a bigger player, like what happens in the financial world."

"You could say that. It's the same old story of every man who has strived to be all powerful. He crushed the competition. He eliminated rivals. He's number one in his gang. There's no number two."

"Then why he's not in prison?"

"Lack of evidence. He's a smart cookie. He operates by fear. He only selects members with families. Every one of them has a vulnerability. He knows their children, parents, siblings, and wives. If anyone dares to double-cross him, he does not hesitate to unload his revenge on their loved ones. No one has snitched on him. He uses encrypted messages. Never ever gets directly involved with crime. He's the modern-day Moriarty."

"Let's give him his match."

"I'm glad to hear that you are in high spirits. Do you need a medical checkup?"

"No. I'm physically fine. Thanks for asking."

"OK, tell me why they released you?"

"I don't know. I was blindfolded and tied and one day I was not."

"What were they saying to you?"

"They were threatening me. Telling me what I had done and what is in store for me. I'm a dead man walking, they said. There were many voices. No idea who they were."

"And then they let you go?"

"Mysteries of life."

I lie with conviction. Staying with kidnappers and criminals has an obvious effect on me. Who you are, depends on the kind of company one keeps. I'm living proof of that. If I ever need to finesse my lying skills, I need to hang out with politicians.

"Have you called anyone?"

"Not yet. My phone is dead. But I'm dying to speak to my parents and girlfriend."

"Be patient. Your phone may be bugged and so maybe the case with your loved ones."

"They can do that?"

"Not only they can but they will. They have a network of ransomware hackers. It's a lucrative business. They have recruited top-of-the line hackers from around the world. Even intelligence agencies fear them. It won't take too long for them to bug your phone. In fact, we should expect it."

"What's the solution?"

"Anti-virus software."

"Excuse me."

"Just kidding. You lie low and stay silent."

"Why would that do?"

"It will give them a false sense of security. They can't track you. Out of sight out of mind."

"How long can I hide? It's not sustainable."

"You have law enforcement behind you. Why worry?"

"It's easy for you to say. It's not the life I want."

"I can understand. But at least do it for a few weeks. We will trap them. Any evidence and Rob is done."

"I'll be the bait. Not a reassuring proposition."

"You can call yourself a bait or a target. Doesn't matter. Let's not quibble with words. They are after you. We want them to attack you at the moment of our liking. We should be the one with the element of surprise, not them."

"Makes sense."

"I always do."

The guy clearly has an elevated sense of worth. I'm not surprised. He's awash in power from head to toe. An alpha male. Nothing can go wrong attitude. Makes me nervous though.

"What's next?"

"Get ready. We need to go."

"Where?"

"I'll tell you on the way."

CHAPTER 36

We are on our way. We pass by Officer Blunt's office. Detective Sheer has no intention of saying goodbye to him. His ego is too big to acknowledge the clumsy officer. He waves goodbye to Lucy, the receptionist. She blushes. Something is cooking here. This guy will do well as a reality TV star. A heartthrob who breaks hearts. I want him to break criminals' heads. Not sure if he's good at that.

There's a black Ford Explorer with tinted glasses parked right in front of the station. No parking sign is hovering next to it. That's what I call attitude.

"You found a good parking spot," I tease him.

He smiles. He likes to show off. Why shouldn't he? If I could, I would too.

He opens the car door for me. I'm pleasantly surprised. A chivalrous guy. That's the first impression. May or may not sustain. He checks the mirror, and seatbelts, and looks all around. A safe driver. Reassuring for me. It shows a caring mentality.

We are out of Banff in no time. It's not Manhattan. It ends before it starts. I know it's hyperbole, but you get the picture. And it's a picture-postcard town. It doesn't have the Matterhorn but a laid-back attitude and warm hospitality more than make up for it. I could sense that in my brief visit to Banff.

Detective Sheer turns West instead of East on the highway.

"Are we not going to Calgary?"

"Nope. We are going to Jasper."

"Why?"

"I can't share all the details due to operational reasons but let's say we are running away from Rob Bank and not running into him."

"Calgary is his home."

"Of course."

"It makes sense. I trust you."

The road Jasper is long and winds around the mountains. It's no Pacific Coast Highway but no less pretty. The ocean is missing but so is the traffic. Nature at its best, free and untouched. Wilderness reminds us how this planet was and still is in some parts of the world. We have become so entrenched in urban and social life that we forget that the earth looks prettier without us. I'm not a hardcore environmentalist. My environmentalism begins at the recycle bin and ends at the organics bin.

We drive in silence. It gets awkward after

a while. Detective Sheer has his eyes on the road which he should but a glance at the beautiful landscape won't do much damage unless he's tailgating someone which he's not. I keep my eyes on the sides of the road, basking in the breathtaking natural beauty of the Rockies.

"Did you always want to be a cop?"

"Not really. I was more fascinated by criminals." He glances at me with a wink.

"Then why didn't you? There are no entry barriers to becoming a criminal." It's my turn to smile.

"But barriers are waiting for you once you become a criminal."

"True. Who do you admire the most?"

"Jack the Ripper."

"What? Of all the people in the world, you admire Jack the Ripper." I frown and throw my judgment at him.

"You took it the wrong way. I thought we were discussing criminals. I admire historical figures Napoleon, Churchill, etc."

"So, you like history."

"Yes, I like history and I remember history. If we forget our history, do you know what will happen?"

"We will repeat it."

"We may but more importantly we will distort it."

"You're well-read."

"Not exactly. I have a subscription to History

Channel."

I give him a thumbs up.

"Tell me what you were doing in Calgary when you caught the drug dealer?"

"I was doing a rotation at the Forensics Institute in Calgary."

"You're working with Dr. Gore?"

"You know him?"

"I don't but I have read about him. You know I am well-read."

"Yes, you are. And yes, I did work with Dr. Gore."

"So, you have interest in the dead?"

"You are bang on."

"We're not too different from each other."

"But we are. You point guns at others and others point guns at me."

"Not anymore till I'm around."

"Thanks."

We drive in silence once again. Our talks happen in bursts followed by long pauses of silence. We are not a couple but behave like one.

CHAPTER 37

Detective Sheer pulls into a plaza. Not any plaza, it's a tourist hot spot, Columbia Icefields. There's a beeline of tourist buses going to the icefield. The icefield is a wonder of nature and people want to enjoy it before it becomes another victim of climate change. Notwithstanding the natural beauty, it's not a place to hide. Is he mad? If we had to stay in a tourist hotspot, what was wrong with Banff?

"Are we going to the icefield?"

"I wish we could. We are going to meet a friend."

"Personal visit?"

"Nothing is personal when I'm on duty. There's a guy who lives here who will help us. He has hidden many people before. It's a reliable hideout place."

"We're staying here?"

"Yes, we are. It's getting dark. I don't drive at night. At least not if I can avoid it. The highway can get narrower, and visibility could be low. On top of that, there is a risk of rocks falling. Better be safe than sorry. Right?"

"But it's a busy place. Do you think it's a good idea to stay here?"

"That's true but the place is going to get deserted once the tourists go and they will soon."

"OK if this is the right thing to do then we'll do it. I trust you."

Shops are closed on the far end of the plaza. There are residential quarters upstairs. We drive behind the plaza. We park there and take the stairs. We reach apartment 101 and knock.

"Come in," a voice says.

We open the door. It's a tiny bachelor's apartment. Oh Gosh! It smells in here. Not a smoke smell, probably weed. The place is bright though. Big windows, there's a good view of the highway and the icefield. There's no bed, only mattresses. No carpet, only vinyl flooring. There's a ceiling fan. No air conditioning. No artwork. All in all, shabby and depressing.

"Hi, Dustin."

"Hi, buddy." His voice is muffled. The volume is low as if someone has dialed it all the way down close to the mute setting.

Dustin gets up slowly. The guy looks emaciated. Maybe he has some chronic health ailment or maybe he doesn't like food. He's barely five feet tall. His hairline is receding. His teeth are rotten. Clothes need a change. The shoes had seen better days. He has a fine tremor on both hands.

And he smells which is separate from the general aroma of the room. His stomach is small, there is a tube coming out of it. The guy has been through a lot.

"This is Karan. He needs help."

"I'm at your service." He waves at me. He takes time to finish his sentence. Not stuttering, only mentally sluggish.

"He will spend the night here and I'll pick him up at 9:00 AM tomorrow."

"You're leaving me?" I'm alarmed.

"There's space for only one in here. I'll find a hotel in a nearby town. I must do some work at night on my laptop. I can't do it here."

"Why can't I go to the hotel with you?"

"That's too risky. You're hiding, remember?"

Bummer. I don't buy his argument, but I don't push him. I have already pushed my luck enough. I am disappointed. Is this how I'm going to hide? How the mighty have fallen. He's going to sleep in a nice hotel, and I am left in a dungeon. Maybe it will be a good experience. Something different. I console myself.

I say goodbye to him. I don't smile. He doesn't either. He knows this place is not ideal for me but there is no choice, I guess.

Me and Dustin. It will be a long night. I sit on a love chair. He sits on a couch. We stare at each other, waiting for the other to start a conversation.

"Do you want something to eat?"

An excellent question from Dustin. He's

redeeming himself but I don't want his home cooked food considering his hygiene.

"Do you have a fast-food place downstairs?"

"Yes, we do. What do you want?"

"I would have a chicken burger with fries. A cold drink on the side. That would be all."

"No problem."

I offer cash.

"I can't accept that. I may not be rich, but I still have some ego left. Food is on me. You are my guest and besides, I'll get it reimbursed."

"OK if that's what you wish."

I don't want to go back and forth with this guy. I barely know him. I don't know if he has anger issues or a criminal background.

I'm alone in the room. I get up and open the window. It's stuck. I use ingenuity to open the window. It takes three minutes of frustration to open it. A fresh cool breeze is coming straight from the glacier. It's a lifesaver in the summer. I check the highway. Tourists are leaving. Sun is setting and shops are closing. I hope he gets my burger.

"Food is here." It's music to my ears.

The food is warm. It's an OK burger. I've had better. A cold drink is a cold drink. Not much imagination there.

The staring begins, someone must break the ice again.

CHAPTER 38

I finish the food. It was fulfilling. I forgot to ask Dustin to eat. Bad manners. It's too late now. He lives here, he should know when to eat or maybe he is fasting. None of my business.

"You are a doctor, eh?"

"Not exactly but hoping to become one."

"I hope you don't mind me saying that, but I am scared of doctors."

"Can I ask why?"

"My doctor scares me more than a Stephen King novel. He once told me, that my eyes would turn yellow, my legs would swell up, my tummy would turn into a football, I would spit up blood, spiders would crawl on my body, my breasts would get bigger, my balls would get smaller, and I would itch myself to death. After this horror show, he dared to ask me if I get annoyed when others talk about my drinking. And do you know what I said?"

"What?"

"I said hell yeah! He tried to stick labels on me. He proclaimed I was alcohol dependent. I always saw my glass as half-full, at least it sounded better than an alcohol abuser. He told me there was a pill to quit drinking. I asked how it would work. He said it would make drinking hell. I would puke if I took a sip."

"Did you take the pill?"

"Thank you very much. I didn't. He wanted me to join support groups. I told him I didn't believe in all this crap. He wanted to suspend my driving license. How could he be so stupid? I didn't even have a car. I only used the license as an ID. He wouldn't budge. He basically wanted to save his ass. I said to him to go ahead if it makes him sleep well at night. I went to him to get the disability form signed. He wouldn't come around to signing it. So much for this so-called patient-centered approach. He said drinking alcohol was not a disease and I did not qualify for work exemption. I was blunt with him, 'Thanks for nothing, doc.' Now you know why I am mad at doctors."

"I can understand your frustration. You went to get empathy but got ridiculed."

"Thank you. It was not just doctors. I expected folks in the drinking business would be sympathetic to my cause, but all I saw were eyes oozing with judgment. I was not asking anything for free. I contributed to their salaries. The money went into the coffers of the government. Wasn't it social service? If they wanted to be preachy, why didn't they become priests? My expectation of the city police was zilch. Their motto was to harass and suspect. I rode a bicycle for heaven's sake. I didn't bother anyone. I was not carrying any illegal drugs. I carried a bottle of alcohol, duly legalized by Her Majesty's Government. I wanted to be left alone, but apparently, that was too much to ask."

"In difficult times, only family can help. Did you have loved ones who held your hand?"

"Speaking of the loved ones, my better half considered herself a lot better. She was not a boxer, yet I was her punching bag. She didn't work for Canada Revenue Agency, yet I had to pay her share in installments. She was not a javelin thrower, yet she managed to hurl insults with remarkable accuracy. It made my skin thick, perhaps that's what Darwin meant by the theory of evolution. I spent all my money on booze. I didn't have any money left for her. She went into a rage. She slapped me. If I wanted, I could have called the police. But would they have believed me? I was already on their naughty list. I felt humiliated. I was too weak to respond in kind. I wanted to die. I threw away the bottle. Thank God, it was empty. She made me clean up the mess. I cut myself doing that. She didn't care. I didn't care either. If I had to die this way, so be it. A drop of alcohol was worth more than a drop of my blood. That was the going rate."

"I suspect you guys are no longer together?"

"You guessed it right. How could I? My bottles would go missing. My wife flat out denied having anything to do with this despicable act. I began hiding them but somehow, she found out. It became a game of cat and mouse. I had to be ingenious to save my prized possessions. I stored alcohol in unmarked containers. It worked. She was furious. I outsmarted her. She didn't give up. She carried out surveillance. I was about to be caught red-handed. She was fast approaching. I had to hide it. The only way was to gulp down."

"Did you?"

"Of course, I did just that. It was the second-worst mistake of my life. I realized it wasn't alcohol. I screamed. I vomited. I fainted. She called the ambulance. I was in the hospital. I was in the operating room. I was in the ICU. I was in rehab."

"Oh God, I am so sorry to hear that."

"I am here now. I cannot drink or eat anymore. I have a feeding tube. Taste is gone, and so is my desire to eat. I cannot speak loudly anymore. It's too bad as I have so much to say. My smile is gone. It has been replaced by a gloomy state. My sleep is gone. That hasn't ended my nightmares. I cannot look at myself in the mirror. The reflection is too painful to watch. There are a lot of things I can still do. I cry. I lay blame. I feel sorry. I feel guilty. I feel ashamed. I get angry. I can become an example for others. I can write, look at me, what have I done? I am in battle with myself, the battle of hope and despair. I have quit alcohol. My liver is healing. I will probably live longer as a result. But do I want to? Do I have to?"

This guy's life is a tragedy. He is ready to

explode and vomit his frustrations all over me. I don't blame him. He blames himself. If I was in his place, I don't know what I would have done.

"Don't give up on life. You have fought hard. It's a tough journey that we all must complete."

"It's easy for you to say. You can't feel what I have been through."

"That's true but I have seen worse. You are at least independent. You don't have to ask for help. Isn't that something to be thankful for?"

"You have a point but when the pain hits you, no amount of consolation works."

"Pain makes you feel alive. I am talking from personal experience."

"Thank you for the sermon. I want to be alive and well." He is trying to elevate his pitch to show displeasure but it's not happening. I back off.

"Are you getting medical care?"

"I already told you I hate doctors. I have taken things into my own hands."

"How so?"

"I take care of my own pain. I make my own cocktail."

"Street drugs?"

"You may call them what you want. They keep me alive."

"But not well."

"That's your perception."

I change the topic.

"How do you know Detective Sheer?"

"The guy gives me the things I want. I am

forever in his debt."

"You mean drugs?"

Dustin is getting restless.

"I'll say no more."

He walks up and down the apartment. He spoke too much. He knows it. I don't know what to make of his revelations. Detective Sheer is being a Good Samaritan or using drugs to keep him under control for use in covert operations.

Dustin prepares the bed for me. The pillows are brown. The quality is great. Nice colors to hide stains.

I get in bed, it's cozy. I'll sleep well. I'm tired. Hope there are no bed bugs.

"Goodnight," I say.

"Goodnight. You're a nice guy. I'll have one piece of advice for you. Guard your front and watch your back."

"Thanks."

Not sure what to make of it. I'm here for only a layover. Why overthink? All will be well.

CHAPTER 39

I'm wide awake before the sunrise. Sleep came in short bursts, but I aggregated five hours of sleep which is enough for me. I was afraid of bed bugs. Those rascals were thankfully absent. What was not absent was the smell from the pillows. There's no free lunch or a sleepover. You pay in annoyance, and I paid that in full.

I use the washroom first. One who uses a washroom first gets a clean washroom. I adhere to that principle. I take a shower. The water is cold, but it awakens my senses. I'm fresh and ready for a new adventure. I come outside. Dustin is awake and staring at me.

"Coffee?"

"Do you have tea?"

"Come on, it's not a fancy place. Black coffee is all I have."

"OK, I'll have some."

The coffee is surprisingly good. He offers biscuits, which is nice of him. They are sweet and crunchy.

"If you ever need my help, don't hesitate to call. I will write my number." It's good form to show gratitude to Dustin. He's been a good host considering his situation.

"I don't think I'll be the one asking for help."

"You never know."

It's eight in the morning. Waiting for someone is not as painful as it used to be. I surf the internet. Dustin reads old gossip magazines.

"You know I always wanted to go to Hollywood." There is glee in Dustin's eyes.

"I've been to Hollywood. You can too if you don't have a criminal record and are eligible to enter the United States. It's not as fancy a place as it is made out to be."

"I'm not talking about visiting. I'm talking about starring in a movie and having my own star on the Hollywood Walk of Fame."

"Oh, you mean the dreams we all have."

"But life had other plans."

"Did you go to drama school?"

"No nothing like that. I joined a construction company. That's the difference between dreams and reality."

"Don't give up. There are plenty of opportunities in Canada. You can go to Toronto or Vancouver. If you don't star in a movie, a sitcom may be around the corner. If that doesn't work out, you can be a character in a novel and you can write it yourself."

"I can do that. Can I make money doing it?"

"Don't bet on it."

"My grammar is bad."

"There's an app for that."

"Thanks for the career advice. Let me give you some advice of my own. Don't take people at face value. They may have not gone to drama school, but they sure can act."

Our conversation is interrupted by a knock on the door. Right on the money. Not a minute past nine.

"Hello fellas, had a pleasant night?"

The detective looks fresh in a blue silk shirt. He hasn't changed his trousers though. I hope he has changed the undergarments. I can see what he's wearing inside but it's too gross to analyze that.

"Fantastic," Dustin says.

I only smile. I have a grudge against the detective. He left me in this rundown place and is teasing me now. He has got the power, so I can't be nasty to him. But I can be passive-aggressive.

"Did Dustin trouble you?"

"No, no. He has been a gracious host."

"Good. Ready to go?"

"Yes, as much as I can be."

There is no luggage, only me. But I do carry baggage but of a different kind. I wave goodbye to Dustin. He offers his hand. Handshaker. I'm missing a sanitizer.

Another beautiful day. The light is reflecting off the glacier, making it brighter. We are on the highway, to hell or heaven we shall see, but there is Jasper on the way.

The drive to Jasper is going uneventful meaning boring and yawn-provoking. Even black coffee is not enough to get the boredom out of me. Nice scenery but once you have seen one mountain you have seen them all. I know it's a terrible thing to say but that's what I'm feeling right now. The detective is keeping his eyes on the road and I'm keeping my eyes on the number plates of cars, looking for interesting patterns. This is how bored I am.

CHAPTER 40

The Welcome to Jasper sign brings in some relief. We drive past downtown into a wooded area. The downtown is small. Expected. I used to like secluded areas but not anymore. Terrible things happen in secluded areas.

"There's nobody around."

"It's Jasper, not Toronto. There are not that many people around here. That's what makes it charming."

We reach a wooden lodge. It's a replica of the lodge I was kept in by the kidnappers. All lodges look alike to me. There's that.

"Whose house is this?"

"A friend. It's a much better hideout. Secluded but luxurious. A different world from Dustin's lodgings."

"I hope you're right. How long are we staying here?"

"I don't know, maybe a few days. Let's go in first. Decisions will be made in due course."

I can see surveillance cameras and a

warning sign: This premise is under 24-hour video surveillance. A good sign in my eyes. It's a big place, 4000 square feet at least. The door is locked. It's an electronic door. The detective puts in the passcode and the door opens. The place is bright and fully furnished. We take the stairs.

I wait for him to show me the way.

"You first," I say.

"You first," he says.

There is some back and forth. I oblige. It's only going upstairs. No biggie. I'm not going to get lost on the stairs.

We enter a big room with at least twelve feet ceiling. There's a chair in the middle. Brown leather sofas on the sides. A ceiling fan is running. Windows are covered with blinds. And there are six people inside staring at me, all with guns in their hands.

"My bodyguards? I don't need that many people to defend me."

"Take a seat," Detective Sheer says.

I sit on the chair. It's heavy, wooden, and uncomfortable.

The two guards block the stairs. Two are behind me. Two guards and the detective face me.

"Are we expecting more?"

I am alarmed but I should trust the professionals. Hopefully, they know what they're doing.

"Yes, we are waiting for our boss," Detective Sheer says.

A man walks into the room. He's wearing sunglasses. He's accompanied by two men with guns. The man stands in front of me and removes his sunglasses. I am not impressed, but he's trying.

Wait a minute. I know this man. He's the boss. Is he the detective's boss? It can't be. He's Rob Bank.

I jump out of my seat. The other men charge at me with guns blazing. Pistols, rifles, semi-automatics, you name it. I'm not a gun guy but all I know is those guns are full of bullets and the fingers are on the trigger.

"Sit down please," Rob Bank says.

He has a soft voice, and it suits his harsh orders. He still looks the same as I remember him. Soft physique and hard resolve.

I sit down. I have no choice. After a few slaps, I can perhaps put up a fight but not against guns. It's game over.

"Are you surprised to see me?"

I am but I am not going to admit it. I keep a poker face.

"Nice to see you again. I'm sorry I didn't introduce myself. I am Rob Bank."

"I know." It's my turn to surprise him.

"How do you know? You were blindfolded when I saw you last." He frowns at me.

"Your men didn't even know how to blindfold properly, and you saw the result."

I rub his ego.

"Do you think you're that smart?"

He bought my lie.

"How can I be smart? I got duped. Since I can't tell a bad cop from a good one, you can call me stupid."

"Stupid you are. I'm not even a cop." The so-called detective interjects

I am stumped.

"You assumed I am Detective Sheer."

"Because you said so."

"Exactly. Perhaps you may also believe that you have a long-distance relative that has left millions of dollars for you somewhere in India. Only if you could give your bank account details."

"You are exactly right. I am stupid but what about others in the police station."

"They are even more stupid. I told them who I was, and they believed me without hesitation. Didn't even bother to check my ID."

"But that doesn't make any sense. How come you arrived at the right place at the right time?"

"There's no mystery here. Good old surveillance and good old luck. I saw you in the parking lot in Banff. We followed you. You didn't recognize me in the souvenir shop. How could you? You went to the police station. It took a couple of compliments to get the receptionist to give us the information. For the rest of the details, you can fill in the blanks."

Rob pats the fake detective. "Good job."

"You acted well, I must say." I give him the compliment as well. He deserves it.

"I took acting lessons. We are professionals. Continued education helps."

"I feel like punching you, but you treated me well. I'll keep that in consideration when I take revenge on you someday."

"Considering your precarious situation, you should worry about your well-being first. My job is done. It's between you and the boss."

He bows in front of Rob Bank and walks away.

CHAPTER 41

I am ashamed. How could I fall for it? I did not take adequate precautions. I lowered my guard. I clicked on the email I was not supposed to click. I believed the online dating profile was nothing but true. I sent my bank account details in a text message in hopes of getting a refund. I responded to a voicemail from Service Canada claiming an arrest warrant may be issued against me unless I clear my account. I am worse than a cybercrime victim. I deserve what I got.

"Most of your guys are idiots but you have some good ones as well."

"Good people are hard to find. And in my profession, it's not that there are hundreds of applicants for one position. There is a perpetual labor shortage. Doesn't matter that I pay way more than the minimum wage."

Rob is enjoying playing with me. I am scared and I should be. It's the worst situation I've ever been in. I don't think I'll make it out alive.

"Are you going to kill me?" The most

important question I ask first.

"Not now. Maybe later. It all depends."

"On what?"

"On your response."

"I don't understand."

"I know people need instructions all the time. I hope you don't need a manual to breathe."

He's a talker. Man, come to the point. But I nod at him. Validation may save my life.

"What do you need from me?"

"Indulgence for the moment. Your balance is in the negative, you need to clear your account."

"You want money?"

"How much can you give me from your piggy bank? You're a medical student, they only have debt."

"So, you have done your accounting."

"All calculations have been done. My brother is in jail. Two of my men were killed in Toronto. Two more lie buried in Banff. That's three strikes for you if you understand sports metaphors."

"You know about the log incident?"

My bad luck never seems to end.

"Of course. There were hidden cameras. I have the footage. You dragged the bodies, didn't you?"

He's bluffing but even if he's not, he can dig up the graves, evidence is right there.

"Are you blackmailing me?"

"I would call that leverage. I know you did a criminal act. If you want to use self-defence as an excuse, then I will play the fear card."

"Sorry."

"You will be when your parents and your girlfriend get into trouble for your actions. I know where they live. I know where they are. You are their well-wisher I imagine."

"You got me by the throat. What do you want?"

"You are an asset. A productive asset. I know you can kill. You have killed four already. Two of them brutally. It means you have criminal potential. I see an opportunity."

"That's a compliment I don't want to get."

"But you can't hide away from your demons. I have a plan for you. You got my brother in jail. You will get him out."

"That's not in my hand. I'm not a judge. I'm not a politician. I can't pardon him. Go talk to a lawyer."

"But you are his out-of-jail card."

"You mean prison break. Are you crazy?"

"Crazy is the new sensible you know. Hear me out. He's being produced in the provincial court. When he comes out, we will snatch him."

"He's not going to be with a kindergarten teacher. There'll be cops. Lots of them with lots of guns."

"Lots is a meaningless number. There will be four cops. We have done reconnaissance."

"Four is plenty. I can't overpower them."

"You will have help. There will be three of

you. One is a runner, and the other one is a street racer. You only need that much."

"Should we overpower them by telling jokes?" I push back. It's risky to confront him but it may be riskier if I keep my mouth shut.

"You'll have a spray. It will do the job."

"Bear spray. Come on. I can already see a problem. What if they close their eyes?"

"It's no bear spray. It's a special cocktail. An anesthetic. You don't need eyes. Nose and mouth only. They will breathe and they will fall."

"What if I breathe the same thing? I will be on the ground and your plan will bite the dust."

"Hold your breath for ten seconds. That's all you need. It's an ultra-fast-acting anesthetic. You can do it, I know. If you can't, I have waterboarding classes available for you to learn."

"Have you ever heard of shock and awe? Why can't we have more people? It will be far easier."

"It won't be. Trust me. More people, more uncertainty, more ways things can go wrong. It's basic probability theory."

He's making some sense. But the operation remains far too risky. Maybe not that much for him but for me, my life is on the line.

"Gary."

Rob summons a man. A short guy, five feet four inches comes forward. He's thin and athletic.

"He will join you. He's sharp with the reflexes of a squirrel. He will be your best new friend."

I don't know about that, but the guy looks promising. My mind is not made up. I should put up resistance. I must push Rob. Let's see where his boundary is. But do I really want to find out? I'm confused.

"I don't have the courage to do this."

"It's a big task. Stakes are high. If you love your family and value your life, you'll do it."

Rob threatens with a calm voice. That shows resolve. That means he's serious. His threat is credible.

"I need time to think."

"It's not a real estate deal. There are no negotiations on a closing date. My brother is being produced in the court tomorrow and there are no second chances. So tomorrow it is."

"Tomorrow!" I need a cold drink to cool down.

"Yup. Eleven o'clock. Downtown Edmonton, provincial court. Be ready."

"Even if we get through the cops. Does your brother know that we're coming?"

"Don't worry about that. You tell him to let's go and he'll know."

"What about the exit plan? You know most criminals die while on the run."

I don't know if it's true, but it feels true and makes my point.

"We have it all figured out. You take a rest in this room. They'll be guards outside. So please don't try too hard. It's not worth it."

"I know."

I'm alone in this room with a mind full of crazy thoughts. Let's see what tomorrow brings.

CHAPTER 42

I can't sleep. My reticular activation system is not shutting down. I'm plotting to get out. I feel like I'm in an abusive relationship. Getting out is not easy, it's downright dangerous. These guys are audacious. I got kidnapped inside the police station. It's the first in Canada's history, I think. There is no safe place for me. They want to ambush the police and get their guy. It shows their confidence. They are not reckless. Rob knows what he is doing. At least that's the impression I have.

Should I save myself or my loved ones?

It's a terrible place to be in. Ideally, I want to do both but I'm afraid I'll be able to do neither. I'm getting into the dirty swamp of crime. I can only go down, not out.

But maybe there is some hope. Rob is angry with me as I got his brother into trouble. If I pay back, maybe he'll let me go. You surrender and you'll be treated humanely. That's what the victorious army tells the losing side. How many of those promises are kept? May history be your guide.

I should prepare for the worst. Wait for my chance. Patience has kept me alive. And my newfound power is a bonus. Maybe I'll get even stronger. Maybe I'll develop new powers. I can't count on it but that's all I have.

I hear a knock on the door. It's seven o'clock already. I didn't realize when I slept. I know I was awake till 2:00 AM. I slept for five hours. Not bad eh.

"Breakfast is ready."

I like the sound of that.

"Coming," I say.

It's not home but I did get a homely feeling even if it was for a second.

I go downstairs. Oh my God, it's a buffet. The breakfast table has everything, bread, biscuits, jam, sausage, eggs, salad, yogurt, juice, tea, coffee, you name it.

I can't decide what I want to eat. That's the problem with buffets. Maybe a little bit of everything.

"Decisions, decisions," Rob whispers in my ear.

"Yup."

"There are perks that come with the job."

He's talking like a recruitment salesman. Come here, it's a dream job. Nice little place, clean and friendly. When you go, only then do you know why no one else wanted it. There's no free breakfast, that's all I know.

I'm in a different position. I'm being drafted. Being sent to a war zone. The option of being a conscientious objector is not available to me.

I pick jam, toast, and orange juice. Keep it simple. Keep it light. There is a high possibility I'll throw up today. I must plan for it.

There are at least seven people in the room. They are eating. No gossip. No laughs. It's like a funeral. I expect no less from these guys who kill for a living.

"If you're done, please go upstairs to the dressing room," a guy whispers in my ear.

I oblige. I sit down on a chair in front of a mirror.

"Make-up time." It is a male hairdresser. He doesn't look like a hairdresser. He looks more like a bouncer. His muscles are as wide as my face. I'm pretty sure he does multitask. Hairdressing cannot be his only job.

He put powder on my cheeks. Hands are rough.

"Really." I give him looks. "I don't need to look pretty."

"Very funny. Please pay attention. It's going to save your life. You want people to recognize you. Do you?"

He has a point. I want to be invisible when I do the crime. If that's not possible then camouflage is in order. I sit and wait as I turn into a white guy. Blonde hair, white face, blue eyes. I can't still see my skin, but I can extrapolate.

"I can't recognize myself."

"Thanks. Job done."

I'm given a suit and a tie. I'm baffled. I thought I'll be in military uniform but here I am looking like a car salesman.

CHAPTER 43

I go downstairs. The other two members of the team are already there. One is in a hard hat and high visibility jacket. The second one in shabby clothes, a fake homeless man. Apparently, this is the guy with the reflexes of a squirrel or rabbit or some fast animal.

"Hi, I am Don," the fake construction worker says.

"Hi, I am Gary. I think we met before," the fake homeless man says.

We shake hands. No hugs. It's not a love fest.

"Why?" I look at Rob Bank. I don't think I need to explain my question.

"Diversity is our strength." He answers like a politician.

The tactic is genius. All different looking guys, no one would think we are related in any way. But I'm still not sure it will be enough. Overpowering a police officer with a gun is no small feat.

We get into the back of a black SUV. Range

223

Rover Sport. I take the back seat.

"It's bulletproofed you know," Gary says.

"Really."

"No expenses spared. We modified it. It's worthy of being in a presidential motorcade."

I don't argue. I was expecting a map or something with detailed plans but so far nothing.

"Where's the plan?" I ask.

"If you know how to spray, we'll be fine," Don says with an attitude.

I shake my head. I don't know if these guys are geniuses or idiots. I'll soon find out.

We reach the outskirts of Edmonton. Traffic is heavy. Only thirty minutes left to reach the destination.

Don presses the accelerator. We are speeding through the bus lane, and school lane, making U-turns. Speeding in a school zone. Horrible.

"Slow down. We will get ticketed." I plead with Don.

"Why'd you care?"

"If we get into an accident I will care."

"Don't worry. I do it every day."

I stop asking questions. He is turning his neck when answering mine. It is reckless and bordering on dangerous. He is not showing any signs of stress. He's chill. He's a professional speedster. He runs a red light. My heart skips a beat. I don't know if I will die of bullet wounds fired by the police, but I'll surely die as a passenger in this car.

He breaks hard in front of the court. My seat belt saves me. Otherwise, my nose would have been history.

"Right on time," Don sounds triumphant.

"What now?" I resume my questions.

"You and I will wait outside. We have reconnaissance in the court. When the target comes out, I'll get a text and we will ambush them." Gary is full of confidence but short on details.

"How?"

"I'll get closer to the police. Asking for money will distract them. And it's then when you fire."

"Fire what?"

"Fire the spray."

"And then?"

"We run."

A child could have come up with this plan. It's simple but I'm not sure it will work. There will be three shots today, all of them mugshots. I'll smile at mine. That's what I expect.

We get out and wait for the police at the bottom of the stairs in front of the court. It's not busy, some clients and lawyers. No crowds though. Gary sits on the stairs. I am twenty feet away from him pretending to check my phone even though it's not charged.

At noon, just as the lunch crowds descend the stairs, Gary winks at me. It's showtime.

I can see four cops accompanying a prisoner.

The cops have normal physiques. No one is above six feet, but they all look agile. Our crew is average too, physically and mentally. No trained boxers or martial artists here. Bunch of amateurs with a veneer of professionalism.

I'll give you an example. Gary is wearing perfume. What the heck. Who would believe that he's a homeless guy? Maybe no one will notice. That's the underpinning behind our plan. To assume that others are bigger idiots than us.

Gary gets up and harasses the officers for money.

"Move away. We are on duty."

I make my move. I get closer to the officers. My hands trembling and my heart pounding. I press the button. I spray the officers. They are in agony, but no one falls to the ground.

"Let's go," Gary shouts at Terry.

"I am cuffed to the cop," Terry replies promptly.

"What are we going to do?" I interject.

"I don't know. I didn't plan for that."

"Great." I'm in full-on panic mode.

Gary is trying to find the key. There are four policemen. It's taking time. It's not happening. Every second is important.

"Hit me. Hit my arms. Forcefully again and again.," I shout.

"What?"

"Just do it."

Gary hits me. Punches, not professional

grade, but what's expected in a street brawl.

I am recharged like an EV. I pull on the cuffs with all my strength and they break.

"Wow."

"It's no time to celebrate. It's time to run," I say and start my sprinting in earnest.

We run. Gary is ahead of me. He's a sprinter. I can't catch him. Even the prisoner is ahead of me. Do you know what it means? I am the first one in the line of fire.

CHAPTER 44

Running is not for me even if it's going to save my life. I'm huffing and puffing, as I haven't run in a while. The other two have more stamina than me. They've been running all their lives. When you are a criminal, that's what you do.

Don is happy to see us. The car is already running.

"Yes!" He can't hide his excitement.

"Let's go," Terry says.

Terry and Gary get in the back. I have to sit in the front. That means I must go around the car. I make a run for it. I hear shots.

"Damn it, they are shooting at us." I am the only one who's not inside the car.

"Come on, get in."

"I know." These guys are not helping.

I open the door.

"Duck, duck," Terry shouts at me.

Bullets hit the car windows shattering glass.

"You said the car is bulletproof," I confront Gary.

"I didn't say it under oath. What are you going to do? Charge me for perjury. Stop wasting time and get in."

My reflexes are not quick. I duck but to no avail. I feel a pinprick sensation in my back. I get in and close the door.

"Are you hit?" Don asks me.

"I don't know. Probably not."

The SUV takes its stride. It accelerates fast but it's not going to outrun a bullet. The shots are being fired but luckily, they miss.

We are on the street, cutting through the traffic. I check my back. There are two holes in my shirt. Round bullet holes. But I don't feel any blood.

"Are you OK?" Don asks again.

"I am fine. You keep your eyes on the road."

"Thank you, guys," Terry says.

"Not yet. We are not out of danger." Gary curbs his enthusiasm.

We enter the underground parking of an apartment building. No signs of police sirens behind us.

"Get out," Gary orders us.

We exit and enter a white Mercedes van.

"Are we going to abandon the car?" I ask.

"It's a stolen vehicle. Why do you care?" Gary responds.

I should have kept my mouth shut. It was stupid of me.

We exit the parking lot. Don is driving again but with less urgency.

"Relax. We are almost there," Gary reassures us.

"Ah! the smell of free air," Terry takes a deep breath.

"How did you manage to break the cuffs and why did you ask me to hit you?" Gary is doing a post-mortem of the operation.

"Secrets of the trade you know."

I try to shut down the interrogation. He is too exhausted to counter my arguments. We reach Jasper in the evening. Mission accomplished.

Rob is waiting for us outside the lodge. He has a bouquet of flowers in his hand. We feel like a victorious army coming back home. Rob greets us all. I'm not talking about just handshakes but hugs.

"Welcome back brother."

"Thank you, brother."

The brotherly hug is extra tight. I am bothered by his hug because you never know what he's up to, but the warmth felt genuine.

Gary and Don have briefcases waiting for them. Rob hands over the briefcases to them. They're full of money.

"It's for you."

"Thank you." Both say in unison.

They open the briefcases in front of him. They smell the dollars. The smell surpasses the best perfume in the world.

"Enjoy the vacation," Rob pats their back.

"We will."

"Lie low."

"We know."

Rob turns to me. "Good job. I'm proud of you. I knew you could pull it off."

"Thanks." I should have said, can I go, but I didn't.

"I'll meet you in the living room. Go upstairs. Get this ghastly makeup off your face."

"I will."

I go upstairs and it takes half an hour for the make-up man to remove it. I join Rob and Terry in the living room downstairs. Terry is sitting on the sofa next to me. There are four bodyguards in the room surrounding us. Rob stands in front of us. The sofa table in front has drinks and dry fruits.

There is champagne and vodka. There's an ice bucket on the side with an ice pick. There are three wine glasses.

"Come on guys, have a drink. It's time to celebrate. Don't hold back." Rob points his hands to the glasses.

"Vodka please," Terry says.

"Of course." Rob makes him a Patiala peg. "Ice?"

"Yes please."

Rob uses the ice pick to crush the ice and pours it into the glass.

"And you?"

"I'll have orange juice."

"Really?"

"Yes please."

"OK if you insist."

Rob gets a glass of champagne, and we all say cheers to a successful mission.

CHAPTER 45

Drinks, nice weather, and a successful mission. There are good vibes in the air. Everything is going well, not for me but for Rob at least. If the boss is happy, you can't be far behind.

"Did you miss me?" Rob asks Terry.

"Of course, brother. I missed you. I missed home. I missed the fresh air."

Rob goes behind his back and massages his hair and cheeks.

"My little brother, I missed you too."

"Thank you for getting me out of prison."

"You're welcome. Do you know who else missed you?"

"Who?"

Rob hands him his cell phone. Terry watches a video. His eyes pop out and his body shivers. Something is trying to come out of Adam's apple. It is stretching the neck like a hatching egg. The icepick comes out of his throat along with the gush of blood. He's making gurgling sounds as he chokes on blood. His head falls backward on the sofa and his body starts convulsing.

I get up from the sofa. I don't know what to say. Surprise and fear. I am surprised at the brutality. If he can kill his brother like this, what is he going to do to me? I fear the unpredictability of this man. Rob is a psychopath.

"The sofa is ruined. The bloodstains can't be removed."

I don't say anything. Neither do the bodyguards. Our poker faces tell it all.

"Take the body and you know what to do with it."

The two bodyguards pick up the body and remove it from the room.

"Call the cleaner."

"Yes Sir."

"Sit down. Relax. It's not your day to die."

I sit down. I keep my eyes on him. I can't let him go behind my back. That's for sure.

"Give me a second. I need to wash my hands. Finish your drink."

I do. I feel like gulping vodka. I need it. My throat is dry. I eat dry fruits as well. Stress induces heartburn. I need antacids but I can't ask for them. I don't know what kind of poison he'll feed me.

Rob is back. His hands are clean, but his intentions are not.

"I know you have many burning questions. Fire away. I don't mind"

I'm in two minds. Is it a trap? Maybe I'll ask. It won't make him worse. He's already at the extreme.

"Why?"

"Good question. Open-ended. Watch this."

He hands me his cell phone. I play a video. Terry is performing a sex act on a woman. I don't want to watch this filth. I hand over the cell phone.

I shrug my shoulders.

"She is my girlfriend. They cheated on me. Terry went behind my back to screw my girlfriend. I did the same to him. Now you understand."

"But he was your brother."

"Only a cousin brother, and dispensable."

"What about your girlfriend?"

Rob gets into a burst of hysterical laughter. Villains do that. It's a cardinal symptom of devilish behavior.

"It's a funny little story. I proposed to her, got on my knees, and offered her the ring. I made her watch the video. Her expressions were priceless. I enjoyed chopping that ring finger and bit by bit, I did the job."

"You got your revenge."

"Isn't revenge sweet. I must thank you. If you had not snitched on Terry, he would not have gone to prison. I would not have got his cell phone and their betrayal would have gone unpunished. They could have killed me. You saved my life in a way."

"But why did you bother to get him out of prison?"

"Do I really need to answer that question?

He was behind bars. I couldn't wait. I wanted instant gratification."

"Congrats, you achieved your objective. Why did you put me through all this?"

"Very good question. It's about you now. Tables are going to turn. I will ask the questions and you will answer."

Oh boy! I have no choice but to answer. But I do have the choice to be discreet.

CHAPTER 46

I am in the hot seat. Interrogation is about to begin. Torture can begin anytime. I have an advantage though. Pain makes me stronger. I want to keep that a secret.

"Do you think I'm stupid?" Rob attacks me from the get-go. Nice tactic.

"I don't know how to answer that question but if I must then I will say no."

I go for the minimum response.

"Good. So, I want you to answer me in a way that does justice to my intellectual abilities." He speaks like a diplomat but has the temperament of a bullfighter.

"I'll try."

"I'll tell you a story. A guy could see something that others couldn't. He spots drugs on a man even though those drugs are planted under the skin which no one else could see. Isn't it something? Then that guy is attacked by two professional killers. He kills them with bare hands even though they are armed. He's kidnapped. He's beaten mercilessly. He somehow breaks free, kills two of his kidnappers, and buries their bodies. He ambushes a police party. Police fire shots at him. Two bullets hit him. There are two holes in his shirt but he's still alive and well and sitting in front of me. Isn't that a miracle?"

"It's sheer luck."

"Nonsense." He pounds his hands on the table.

"I'm telling the truth."

"You better come up with a plausible explanation."

Rob gets a pistol and points it at me. He's bluffing. He won't kill me. He needs me. I know it's wishful thinking, but I need those wishes.

"10, 9,8,7….," Rob begins the countdown.

"I am telling the truth." I stick to my guns.

Bang, bang, bang. Three bullets hit me. All bounce right off me. One bullet glazes Rob's arm. The other goes through the window and the third one goes into the wall.

Rob puts on the handkerchief to stop the bleeding from his arm.

"Need help."

Rob looks at me with disbelief. I pick up a towel and press on his wound to stop the bleeding. Rob gets a knife out of his back pocket and stabs me in the right flank. The knife gets bent.

"What the heck?" Rob sounds angry.

I push him to the ground. The two bodyguards grab me by the arms. Rob gets a spray out of his briefcase from underneath the side table and comes closer to me.

"Now you will speak the truth."

I am on the sofa. Same room. I don't know what happened. I do know I was sprayed but after that, I'm at a loss. It couldn't have been that long. Sun is still not set. I'm groggy. I feel as if I have come out of a deep coma. I've been there before, after the head injury but this feels qualitatively different. I can't pinpoint but I can sense it.

"Now I know everything," Rob boasts to me.

"Good for you."

"It will be."

"Now can you please let me go?"

"I can't. You are my golden goose."

"I don't have any gold to give you."

"But you have something far more valuable, knowledge."

"If you know what I know then you must know that I don't know how I got to be who I am."

"That's a tongue twister. I know one thing. Never ever punch you."

Rob touches my skin. He feels the texture. Sensual or not, his touch is making me uncomfortable.

"I want this skin. I want this body."

"I can't give you that. You are you and me is me."

"But you can share."

"What do you want?"

"You got infected with something. The body

you examined in the autopsy room started it all. Where's that body?"

"It's buried. I don't know where."

"You better find out. I need that body. I need the power."

"I can understand. You want to be all-powerful. Why do you need me? Get the damn body. Kiss it, lick it. I don't care."

"You are coming with me. You will be my scientific advisor. I need someone who has gone through the process."

"What if I don't?"

"You want me to spell out what I'll do to you and your loved ones? Have a look at this live feed."

I see the video on the phone. My parents are sitting on the sofa in a room. My girlfriend is also there.

"Where are they?"

"They are my guests. It's up to you how well they get treated."

I can't say I'm shocked. It was expected. He has chosen the nuclear option. I don't have a credible deterrence. If I have to save myself and my loved ones, I must kill him. I need a chance and I will get it.

"I will cooperate but if anything happens to them, I'll rip you apart one organ at a time."

I make my own threat. Psychopaths only understand the language of threats.

"You have my word."

I can't take his word for granted but that's

his final offer. I'll accept it for now.

"What do you want me to do?"

"Tell me the deceased patient's address."

"I already told you I don't know. I will have to go back to the hospital to find out. Do you want me to do that?"

"Why don't you access hospital records remotely? You must have login information. I know you do. I have worked in the same health system before. I know how it works. Use it."

Damn it. The guy is smart and resourceful. That's why he is a mafia boss.

"Even if I log in, the IP address will be detected. Would that be acceptable to you?"

"Don't worry. We do it all the time. We have tricks. You log in please."

Rob hands me a laptop. I log in. Access is still working. I note down the patient's address.

"Excellent. Did this guy ever use drugs?"

"Yes, he did. He was in rehab before."

"Then we'll find out about him."

Rob makes a phone call. "I want to know where this guy is buried. You have thirty minutes."

Rob runs a syndicate. He has collaborators everywhere. Surrey is no different.

"You didn't finish your drink." Rob turns his attention back to me.

I am skeptical of the drink. What if it's poisoned? I'm no different than Brezhnev who was wary of the drink offered by Nixon.

"I don't want it."

Rob doesn't insist. It means the drink is probably harmless.

"OK if you insist, I'll drink." I change my mind and gulp it. Nothing has happened so far. Fingers crossed.

CHAPTER 47

Rob sits on the sofa. Stretches himself. The bloodstains are still visible on the sofa. He puts a pillow on it and rests his head. He has no remorse. He is proud.

"How does it feel to have superpowers?"

"It doesn't feel that good."

"Why not?"

"Superpowers are overrated. You can see for yourself. What's my situation and what's yours."

"That's because you lack situational awareness. I'll be different."

"I don't know if these powers are transferable."

"They better be."

Rob has high hopes and plans for world domination. He will fall hard under the heavy load of expectations. That's the fate of narcissism.

Rob gets a call back in fifteen minutes.

"Yes. What's the news?" His voice has the excitement of a child looking for a Christmas gift.

He listens. He gets up and throws away his

phone.

"I can't believe it. That rascal got cremated, not buried."

Rob can't take no for an answer. But he can't change the fact. He is pacing in the room. He's thinking. I can tell. I can also see. The blood is flowing to his brain at an accelerated pace.

"What are you going to do?"

"I have an idea. Show me the police report. I want the exact location of his death."

I must log in again. The police report is scanned and available to see and print. It's barely legible but the address is written in capital letters.

"Print it."

"I am breaching patient confidentiality, you know."

"That's the least of your worries."

He's right. I must remain alive to have any career. I print the report and give it to him.

"Now what?"

"We're going there."

"But it's not a walk in the park. It's in the middle of a forest."

"Yeah, but not too far from here."

"We can't take the car. It's deep in the woods. I'm not a professional hiker."

"We are not driving. We are flying."

"There's an airport in Banff?"

"We don't need an airport to land. We are going to be dropped from above."

This guy is crazy. He's going to kill himself

and me.

"I don't know how to use a parachute."

"Google it. Watch a video. And if you have any superpowers, you may survive the fall."

"That's suicidal."

"I don't think so. You practice your parachute skills. You will be given a dummy parachute. We will begin our adventure at 6:00 AM sharp tomorrow. And don't try anything silly to sabotage my plan. You know what the stakes are. You are dismissed."

He speaks like a commanding officer. But I am no professional soldier. I'm a reluctant conscript who's ready to bail out at any moment.

I take the stairs. Rob calls me from behind. "I'll be watching you."

Surveillance cameras must be everywhere. They are not visible, but I know they are somewhere. I can't get a break. One problem after another. I don't want this power. Simple and mundane life is underestimated. I crave an inconsequential existence.

One thing I don't crave is a good night's sleep. No matter what difficult circumstances I am in, I seem to fall asleep. Mental evolution at work. I am sure people slept during air raids in wartime. At least some of them. I can relate to them somehow.

It's 5:00 AM. There's a knock on the door. Someone keeps knocking. It's annoying.

"Yeah, I know it's time. I'll get ready."

That shuts down the voice. But not my problems. They are about to enter an exponential phase.

I take twenty minutes to get ready. Quick shower and bowels are on the clock thanks to anxiety.

I go downstairs expecting a buffet. The breakfast table has cutlery but no food.

"No buffet?" I stare at Rob.

"Only granola bars. I don't want you to throw up. An empty stomach is good for jumping off a plane. We will have packed food available but that's for later."

I eat one granola bar. I drink tea with cream. Some calories can't hurt today. Rob takes black coffee with no sugar. Kind of expected of him.

We take the Mercedes S-class to the airport. Driving in luxury and soaking up the bumps. We reach the airport in ten minutes. When I say the airport, it's a bunch of air hangers and a small airstrip. A small private jet is waiting for us.

"How did the pilot agree to do this?"

"I know what he is afraid of. Besides, he gets boatloads of money."

"Carrots and sticks."

"Exactly."

There is no airport security screening. It's a private airport. Own rules, and liability. We take our seats. There are three of us in the cabin. The third one is to open the door for us to jump. Extra restraints are available to him. He's at risk of falling. And he can't let that happen if he wants to live. He's a young man in his 20s. He's taking risks in his life. This is the age when you think you are invincible. He has a history of cracked ribs. Looks like he didn't learn anything from it. Life may not give him another chance. But that's not my problem.

The pilot acknowledges us and welcomes us on board. He's not smiling. Can't blame him. He desperately wants this to be over with and so do I. He must be in his 50s. Experienced but vulnerable. Rob knows his weak spot and he's putting his career at risk. What's not at risk is the flying conditions. The weather is clear. I wish it wasn't. The flight is a go.

CHAPTER 48

The plane is airborne. There is no in-cabin service. We are staring out of the windows.

"It's forest fire season," Rob says.

"Any fires nearby?" I'm obviously concerned.

"Don't know. Let me check the weather map."

"You didn't check earlier. I can't believe it."

"Relax. There's no smoke nearby. If there was, the pilot wouldn't have flown. But I'll still double-check on the weather app."

"Do it, please. I don't think my power can fight a forest fire."

"I checked it. We are all clear."

"But things can still happen. What if a fire starts when we reach the forest?"

"Probability is quite low."

"But not zero."

"In my line of business that's always the case. Low is good enough. If I start worrying about low probability events, I would be homebound."

My destiny is entangled with him. I can't

wish him bad luck. I pray for our collective safety.

"I'll yell at you when the time comes to open the parachute."

"What if I don't hear?"

"You better keep your ears open. Your life depends upon it," Rob plays with his hysterical laughter.

"We are at the spot," the pilot announces.

I could see a pile of rocks on the side of Bow River. It's ground zero.

"He fell off one of the cliffs around here, didn't he?" Rob asks.

"Yes, you have read the report."

"There's a gap in the forest over the cliff. It's a good spot to get dropped," the pilot announces.

Rob stands up. I follow. The third guy opens the side door. The wind is strong. The plane is hit with heavy turbulence.

"Jump," Rob shouts.

I hesitate. He pushes me. I am in freefall. Weightlessness is a strange feeling. I don't like it one bit. I avoided bungee jumping all my life. But I didn't know that one day I'll be jumping off a plane all on my own. The wind slows me down. I'm beginning to like it. The body that's free of any burden. Freefall gave Einstein the happiest moment of his life. It was through a thought experiment. I am also conducting an experiment of sorts. But I'm no Einstein. The curvature of spacetime is not going to do any favors to me. I'll hit the ground with an acceleration that can be accurately determined. But what is uncertain is my fate.

Rob comes closer to me in flight. He touches my hand, "Now."

I pull on the parachute handle. So does he. I descend at a manageable pace. I fall to the ground. Not a smooth landing but it could have been worse. My body is still intact. Maybe some scrapes on the skin which I can't see anyways. Rob lands on his feet. He has done it many times.

"We made it."

"I told you so," Rob pumps me. He is trying to cheer me up as I am a reluctant participant, and we have a long journey ahead of us.

Rob has a big backpack. Mine is half his size. He's the boss. His needs are more than mine.

"It's hot. Do you need sunscreen?" Rob shows some consideration towards my welfare. It's superficial and selfish, I know that.

"No thanks. My brown skin will protect me."

"Don't be stupid. Brown or white, the sun shines equally on everyone."

I'm surprised to hear those wise words from a psychopath.

"I have a hat."

"OK if you fancy a sunburn. Now remember if you encounter wildlife, just yell. I have a gun in case we need it."

"I have fought a grizzly bear with my bare hands. I think I can handle it."

"That's the kind of power I want."

"What good would that do? You have enough power as it is."

"What power do I have? Hiring a bunch of goons and firing some guns can make me seem powerful but I remain vulnerable and paranoid. I don't even know if I'll see the end of the day. I live in constant fear."

I can't make him give up on his power trip. We are walking aimlessly. It's tough terrain. I have hiking shoes. But my plantar fasciitis is not doing me any favors.

"What are you looking for?" I ask.

"You tell me. I'm not the one who has the power. You got blessed with that green bubbly stuff."

"Maybe we should poke the trees to see if that green stuff comes out."

"Now that's a brilliant idea."

Rob gets a Swiss knife and starts poking.

"Would you mind helping me out as well?"

"You need the treasure, not me?"

"But you are stuck with me. If I don't get the treasure you're not going home. So at least be helpful. Take my bag. That's the least you can do."

The backpack is heavy. I shot myself in the foot. I should have taken the offer to poke trees. It is a less laborious job but it's too late now.

We wander aimlessly for one hour. Nothing but dry bark.

"What if we don't find anything?"

"Failure is not an option."

Rob is obsessed with success. His slogans are more suited to a political campaign. He's going to starve me to death.

"What if it gets dark?"

"We sleep in the forest."

"We have a tent?"

"Only sleeping bags."

"That's horrendous."

"That's why we must find what we're looking for before the sunset. Pick up your pace."

Ambition has turned him blind. I can see that.

CHAPTER 49

The ground is wet and cold due to rainfall yesterday. It's slippery. We tread carefully making even slower progress.

"We're not making any headway. Let's take a break. I am hungry." I have given up already. It's not a surprise as my motivation is low. I'm doing this against my will.

"OK will take a break. Where do you want to sit?"

"I see a flat set of rocks over there. It's a good place to sit. There's shade as well."

"Let's go."

The rocks are 200 yards away. We sit on them and eat granola bars. Concentrated orange juice quenches our thirst. I like the sugar high.

"It's time for a siesta."

"Absolutely not. Ten minutes max. Get your rest and move. We have miles to go."

I stretch my legs on the rocks. I stare at the overhead tree, examining it carefully. I have time to kill. I'm learning botany skills on the go. I notice something weird. The leaves look different. There are broad and spiky leaves on the same tree. I'm not sure what kind of tree it is. Maybe a birch. All I know is you can't have different types of leaves on a single tree. I point it out to Rob.

"Have you seen anything like it before?"

"No, I haven't."

I look around. Something is not right. Leaves are not blowing in the wind. There are no insects or any animals we could see in the trees. There are trees, there is us, and there is silence.

"I don't have a good feeling about it."

"Don't be melodramatic. I'm feeling good about it. Maybe this is the place we were looking for. Let's poke around."

The difference in leaves is subtle, you must look for it like finding atypical moles on the skin. The aberration in leaves is hidden. The ratio of broad to spiky leaves is 20 to 1. Only an astute observer can spot it. I'm not saying I am one, but I got lucky.

Rob digs in the knife. No green stuff comes out but there is a movement of leaves as if they are reacting to the stimulus, like a living organism.

"Damn it, still no luck."

Rob is getting frustrated. He takes out a big army knife.

"I'll ram it in. Maybe the green stuff is hidden inside."

We come off the rocks. There's a downhill path on the other side. We follow it for about a hundred yards. It ends at a pond. I touch the water. It's warm. There's no sign of life in the water. No fish, no insects.

I look across the pond and I can't believe what I see.

"Are you seeing what I'm seeing?" I tap Rob.

Rob turns around. "How is this possible?"

There's a grand banyan tree across the pond with branches scattered for hundreds of feet. We follow the edge of the pond to reach the banyan tree.

"It's a miracle, isn't it?" I can't take my eyes off this wonder of nature.

"Yes, it is. I think we have reached our destination." Rob's eyes are beaming with pride and greed.

The banyan tree is not just a tree, it's an ecosystem. Its thick roots are running deep into the pond. I can see inside the tree. It's a first for me. There are millions of fine structures inside. They are illuminated as if electricity is passing through them. Neurons? What else could they be?

I sit on one of the thick roots of the tree. I follow the roots into the pond. The surface of the pond is soft. My eyes can penetrate it. There are hundreds of skeletons buried beneath. Some I can recognize. Some I can't. There are completely intact skeletons. I can recognize dinosaurs, elephants, and whales. What is this place? Some sort of graveyard for ancient extinct species. The roots of the banyan tree are reaching the skeletons.

The space is filled with fluid. It's thick like soup.

I hear a noise. It's a shrill voice. A scream.

"Did you scream?" I ask Rob.

"No, I didn't. I thought it was you."

Rob has his military knife dug into the banyan trunk.

"Look it's the green stuff we were looking for." Rob puts the green liquid on his finger and is about to lick it.

"Are you going to drink it?"

"No, I'm going to inject it." He takes a ten-cc syringe and fills it up with the green liquid.

"If something happens to you, we don't have any medical treatment available here."

I show a fake concern for Rob's health. I don't give two hoots about if he dies or lives.

"I'm not going to do it here and now. We will go back and do it in a controlled setting."

"What if the green liquid gets clogged?"

"Then we will come back. We know the source now."

Rob takes out the knife. The green stuff stops oozing. The opening closes. There's a hustling noise. The branches of the banyan tree have sneaked up on Rob. His limbs are encircled by the branches.

He's in shock. He freezes.

"What's happening?" I shout.

"These branches are all over me. Like an insect's tentacles."

Rob takes his knife out and starts cutting

the branches one by one. It makes things worse. The branches tightened their grip. He is unable to move. He is being squeezed.

I am seven feet away. I look around me. I've been spared by the branches thus far.

"Get out of here." I give unsolicited advice.

"I can't."

Rob screams. One of the branches has punctured his antecubital vein. The blood is sucked out of him. His blood vessels are drained completely. It takes no more than 20 seconds. His pale body with mouth open and eyes closed falls to the ground and slips into the pond. His skin dissolves as if it has been immersed in sulfuric acid. His body organs float away, leaving only the skeleton. The body organs become a part of the evolutionary soup. The skeleton joins the other hundreds of skeletal specimens that form the bed of the pond.

I am left holding the bag, Rob's bag. I wish I could have recorded the incident. It is the scariest thing I've ever seen in my life. The recording would have been an instant Halloween classic. It's too late now.

The only thing I can do now is run. I do a sprint. Not so fast. I fall on the ground. I get tripped by the branches. They are everywhere on the ground like a spider web. It's my turn to face the onslaught. The branches grip my both legs. I don't fight back. I look at the banyan tree and smile. I don't know why I did that. Maybe if it's a living and breathing thing, I need to make friends not enemies. A smile goes a long way in making friends.

It does no good. The branches poke me. They try to get into my veins. They can't get through. The struggle continues for five minutes. They are the longest five minutes of my life. I now understand the relative meaning of time.

The branches eventually stop poking. I look towards the banyan tree. The nerves inside the tree are lit up. It's like Christmas inside. What I expect is forgiveness.

"I mean no harm. I am part of you. You know why. I won't bother you ever again. Please let me go."

I see some movement. I am being dragged. Faster and faster. Through the woods, through the rocks. The branches release me. I am thrown in the air like a slingshot.

I go over the cliff. I'm falling and falling. Ever so faster every second. Precisely according to the gravitational acceleration. There's no mercy expected from the laws of physics.

I do expect mercy from my fate. There's not too much time to think. I land on the rocks. I bounce like a football. Five feet at least. I feel the impact which means I am still alive. My head is not crushed open. My limbs are intact. So is my ability to see inside. All in all, I escaped unscathed.

I thank my luck. But luck has not always been on my side. The last month has been nothing but a nightmare for me. And the worst part is that it's not a dream but a reality that I can't escape from. But I have met adversity with courage. I should be proud of that. Pep talk is making me feel a bit better.

I gather my belongings but not my thoughts. Those are in a suspended state of disbelief. I can't believe what happened. It will take time to process it.

I open the backpack. I see Rob's cell phone there. It is password protected. I try Bankonme. It works. My luck is on a roll. I have cheated though. I had seen Rob open his cell phone. I knew some words but not the whole combination, that's where the luck got me through.

I search in the messages. There's a live webcam with my parents and girlfriend. They look well, eating breakfast.

I message: Release them.

Acknowledge.

The response comes: Received and done.

I have a burden lifted off my shoulders. My loved ones are safe. I'm relatively safe. I look around. This is the spot where the body was found. I can find my way out of here.

I see two paths going forwards. One is flat but convoluted, and the other one is straight but steep. I know which one I'll take. I begin my journey knowing the path but not knowing the destination. That's life.

ABOUT THE AUTHOR

Preetinder Rahil

Preetinder Rahil writes fiction, non-fiction, and poems that rhyme. He tries to keep things simple, fun, and worth your time. If you have any feedback, please let him know. Listening to his audience will only let him grow.

Twitter: @preetpoet

Made in United States
North Haven, CT
02 April 2023

34926767R00159